BY MICHAEL de GUZMAN

Melonhead

Beekman's Big Deal

The Bamboozlers

Finding Stinko

Henrietta Hornbuckle's Circus of Life

Henrietta Hornbuckle's
CIRCUS OF LIFE

Henrietta Hornbuckle's
CIRCUS
~*~ OF ~*~
LIFE

MICHAEL de GUZMAN

Farrar Straus Giroux

New York

www.fsgkidsbooks.com

Library of Congress Cataloging-in-Publication Data
De Guzman, Michael.
    Henrietta Hornbuckle's circus of life / Michael de Guzman.— 1st ed.
        p.   cm.
    Summary: Twelve-year-old Henrietta Hornbuckle and her parents perform as
clowns in a tiny, ramshackle traveling circus until a family tragedy jeopardizes
Henrietta's whole offbeat world.
    ISBN: 978-0-374-33513-7
    [1. Clowns—Fiction.   2. Circus—Fiction.   3. Family life—Fiction.
4. Death—Fiction.   5. Grief—Fiction.]   I. Title.

PZ7.D3655He 2010
[Fic]—dc22

                                                          2009013602

To W. A.

Henrietta Hornbuckle's
CIRCUS OF LIFE

CROSSING TO THE OTHER SIDE

She stood at the stern of the ferry as it pulled away from the Connecticut shore. Her pale green eyes were fixed intently on the conning tower of the nuclear-powered submarine that was heading home to the naval base up the Thames River. She could just barely make out the hump of its back. It looked like a fake whale, she thought. She knew people lived in its belly for long periods of time. Ixnay had told her so. Ixnay taught her about the machines of the world. She tried to imagine what it would be like to live inside an enclosed place that was sealed shut, but she couldn't. It didn't matter that Ixnay had told her the food on submarines was good. A lot of ice cream. She loved ice cream, but not that much.

Henrietta needed an open window, like the one she was looking through now. She enjoyed watching the world pass by. That's how it had always been, that's how it would always be. She had the best life of any twelve-year-old on the planet. How could that not be true? She was a clown. So was everybody she lived with. She was aware of life outside Filbert's Traveling Clown Circus. She knew that most people lived in houses or apartments. And that they traveled to get to work, and returned each night to the same place. She'd never been inside a house or an apartment. She'd never attended school. She'd never been taught by anybody who didn't love her. Hers was an existence of freedom and movement. Who had it better than that?

 4

She felt the ferry's steel-plated deck vibrating beneath her feet as its old diesel engine hammered away below. She saw the submarine surface in the distance. It looked like a bathtub toy as it entered the river. New London, Connecticut, became indistinguishable from the surrounding countryside. She moved to the front of the boat. She always did at this point in the crossing.

Glances followed her as she went. Her fine, almost white blond hair was in a ponytail, held in place with a ribbon. The color depended on her mood. Today it was red. Her nose was slightly too large for her features, which were themselves slightly too close together, giving her face a comic effect, even when at rest. Her body was roundish. She smiled a great deal because she was happy a great deal of the time. The smile produced a dimple in her right cheek. She was wearing black and white checked shorts, a red bowling shirt, and flip-flops. Altogether she appeared to have been constructed for the sole purpose of providing entertainment, which was fine with her.

So far the summer was going well, she thought. True, business was off. Everybody talked about it. A lot lately. But she was certain that more people would start coming to see them perform soon. Business would pick up. It always did. That was the nature of their lives. It was ups and downs. What pleased her was that she'd improved as a clown. She was better this year. She was stronger. Her timing was sharper. She was learning the exact size to make a gesture to get the biggest laugh. Her father had promised to teach her a new routine. She loved it when that happened. Ahead lay Long Island and a series of performances that would lead them to Manhattan, where they would be part of a Labor Day festival in Union Square.

The five aging recreational vehicles and one overburdened truck that would get them there were both transportation and home for Filbert's Traveling Clown Circus. The RVs were washed-out white, with faded clown faces and balloons on their sides. They were boxy and set on narrow tires, and they all leaned this way or that on springs that had little memory of resilience.

After Labor Day the circus would head south to the panhandle of Florida, then across Alabama, Mississippi, Louisiana, Texas, New Mexico, and Arizona, to California. From there they would perform their way north to Washington, then hook a sharp right-hand turn and make their way east along the northern tier of states on the heels of spring. A year from now they'd be on this same ferry. She sensed somebody at her side and looked up.

"You must be the one and only Henrietta Hornbuckle," her mother said. Hortense had strawberry blond hair and blue eyes and was wearing a yellow sleeveless dress. She was five feet nine inches tall.

"That's me," Henrietta responded.

Her mother smiled. She closed her eyes and put her face to the sun. It was August. The temperature was in the eighties. Long Island Sound sparkled.

"We're going to visit my sister, Carlotta," Hortense said.

This was big news to Henrietta. She knew she had an aunt, but it wasn't something her mother had ever talked about much. This was the first she'd heard of a visit.

"I thought she didn't like you," Henrietta said.

"Before that we liked each other a lot," Hortense replied.

"Where does she live?" Henrietta asked.

"Oyster Bay," Hortense said.

Another news bulletin. They played Oyster Bay every summer. Nobody had ever told her. "Do you think she came to see the show?" Henrietta asked.

"I don't know," Hortense said. "I doubt it. I only found out last year she lived there."

"She stopped liking you because of my father," Henrietta said. "Because you married him and joined the circus."

"She should be over it by now," Hortense said.

"You're still married to my father. You're still in the circus."

Hortense laughed. "It wasn't my fault," she said.

Henrietta liked hearing the story of how her parents met. "You came to see the show."

"I sat in the first row."

"You saw my father and that was that."

"I didn't stand a chance," Hortense said. "He swept me off my feet. But Carlotta and I are all that's left of my family. It's time we patched things up. And I want her to meet you."

Before she could ask her mother why, Henrietta saw her father. Morris Mortimer Hornbuckle, known to one and all as MoMo, stepped lightly down the steel stairs from the cabin deck. His hair was the color of early wheat. His eyes were green. He was wearing jeans, a white T-shirt, and sandals.

"Is this not the most glorious day possible?" MoMo exclaimed as he moved to stand between his wife and daughter.

Henrietta marveled at the sight of her father. She thought him perfect, with the head of a Greek god, the body and confidence of a weight lifter, and the heart of a lion. They were exactly the same height, which was four feet, three inches.

BRING ON THE CLOWNS

Behold," MoMo said, pointing to the tip of the North Fork of Long Island. "Behold the gateway to our first appearance in New York City. You have to love life when you're about to play the greatest stage on earth."

Henrietta had never really been there. She'd only come as close as the bridges and highways the circus traveled to get from Long Island to New Jersey. She thought of Manhattan and its giant buildings as an enchanted place, like the Emerald City in *The Wizard of Oz*.

"We'll start rehearsing the Eight-Foot-Tall this afternoon," MoMo said. "Union Square will be the world premiere."

"What's the Eight-Foot-Tall?" Henrietta asked, knowing that it was the promised routine but not what it was.

"You plus me, dear girl," MoMo said. "Right now we should drink in the moment. Could life be any sweeter?"

They were joined in rapid succession by the rest of the company. Henrietta watched them make their way down the steel stairs. She'd known them all her life.

Wilhelmenia, widow of the late great clown Filbert, owned and operated the circus. She was an enormous woman in red shorts, blue suspenders over an orange shirt, red high-tops, and a Panama hat.

Sweetpea, Wilhelmenia and Filbert's daughter, came next. She was fifteen and took after her deceased father, who'd had an unfortunate accident while riding a unicycle on his head. She was tall and thin. Headphones were clamped to her ears. She was dressed in jeans and a T-shirt with sparkles.

Henrietta liked Sweetpea, despite the fact that Sweetpea did everything she could to avoid acknowledging Henrietta's existence.

Grandmother Spangle, Wilhelmenia's mother, was amazingly agile for ninety-two. Once she'd been part of a nearly famous trapeze act called the Flying Maraschinos. She wore pink pedal pushers and a flowered shirt.

Peppy and Wanda wore shorts, T-shirts, baseball caps, and sunglasses. They'd been juggling together for fourteen years. Wanda was nine months pregnant. Her child would be born any day.

Lola and Guillermo were in their sixties. Before becoming clowns they'd been dance instructors on cruise ships sailing to the Caribbean. Guillermo wore an old wrinkled suit, Lola a silver dress.

Ixnay, Grouchy, and Notz, the Landorini brothers, were last to arrive. They wore matching blue jumpsuits with short sleeves. The Landorinis did a tumbling act and most of the circus's heavy lifting.

"How do you think we're going to do on Long Island this year?" Guillermo asked when they were all lined up at the rail.

"We're going to do great," Henrietta said.

"Better times are coming," MoMo said.

"We didn't do so hot in New England," Peppy said.

"We did great in Rhode Island," Henrietta countered.

"Rhode Island is small," Grandmother Spangle said.

"Nobody cares if we perform on Long Island or the moon," Sweetpea said, momentarily unplastering her headphones. "We're not real clowns. Real clowns perform in real circuses."

"Nobody cares? Nobody cares?" Henrietta snatched the ever-present hats from the billiard ball heads of the Landorini brothers and juggled them. The brothers wore the hats inside and out. Henrietta had seen the brothers sleeping in them.

"Nobody cares if we come or go," Henrietta sang, "nobody cares until they see the show." She took quick measure, then tossed Ixnay's bowler toward its owner's head. Ixnay made a slight adjustment, and the hat made a perfect landing.

"People pay money because we're funny," Henrietta sang. She threw Grouchy's fez, and it scored a bull's-eye.

"They pay and they stay because they laugh when we play," Henrietta sang. She threw Notz's straw boater, and it floated through the air and landed on target. Bowing to the applause, she caught a quick glimpse of Sweetpea smiling.

11

The ferry passed through the churning waters known as Plum Gut. The clowns made their way down to the car deck and climbed into their RVs: Wilhelmenia, Sweetpea, and Grandmother Spangle into the first; Henrietta, Hortense, and MoMo into the second; Peppy and Wanda into the third; Guillermo and Lola into the fourth; Grouchy and Notz into the fifth. Ixnay slid in behind the wheel of the truck.

Hortense started the engine. She did the driving. MoMo was too easily distracted to be any good at it, and she liked the job. Henrietta strapped herself into the single seat directly behind and midway between her parents. She could see the road ahead, and the landscape to either side. Behind her were the tiny kitchen, a small table with three chairs, the half-couch that also served as her bed, the table and mirror where they made up, a tiny bathroom, and Hortense and MoMo's bedroom, which was so small the mattress took up the entire floor space. Boxes were stored on racks above and in trunks secured to the floor. These held costumes, props, and accumulated family possessions. There wasn't much room to move around.

The ferry nudged its way into the dock at Orient Point.

"We're going to do boffo on Long Island," MoMo said.

"Long Island won't know what hit it," Henrietta said.

"We're going to visit my sister when we get to Oyster Bay," Hortense said.

Henrietta looked quickly at her father and saw that he was momentarily speechless.

"After us, Carlotta is the only family Henrietta has," Hortense said, taking advantage of her husband's silence. "She's going to meet her and there's nothing to discuss."

Recorded calliope music exploded from the speaker on top of Wilhelmenia's RV, making it impossible for the conversation to continue. But Henrietta knew it wasn't over.

The ferry crew cleared the gate away, and the caravan that was Filbert's Traveling Clown Circus drove off.

SETTING UP

enrietta, MoMo, Sweetpea, Peppy, Notz, and Guillermo cavorted down the main street of Greenport in frizzy wigs, hats, bulb noses, makeup, and baggy pants. The caravan followed, going about one mile an hour. They did this in every town they played. Advance notice of their arrival was sent to local newspapers, but it was the grand entrance that drummed up most of their business. Since they returned at approximately the same time each year, people knew they were coming. The clowns gave away a few tickets to prime the pump. They did their best to make the children they came upon laugh.

Grandmother Spangle's voice could be heard alongside the calliope music as she barked the time and place of tonight's show over another of the RV's speakers. A young cop yelled at them to hurry it along because they were holding up traffic. MoMo linked his hands in front of him, lifted

Henrietta, then flung her into the air. Henrietta tucked her knees to her chest, spun herself into two neatly executed somersaults, and landed squarely on her feet. Together, father and daughter walked on their hands. They gave out a few more tickets, including a pair to the young cop.

A half hour later the caravan pulled into a field outside town. They formed the RVs into a loose circle along its back edge. This gave them a courtyard of sorts in the middle, a space free from the public eye. It was Lola's turn to cook. She made pasta shells and tossed them in olive oil, garlic, and smushed tomatoes that she'd picked up for a good price because they were going soft.

When lunch was ready, the clowns lined up. Grandmother Spangle was first, an honor accorded her because of age. Lola served them each a plateful. Iced tea, water, and bread were already on the long table at which they ate and held their meetings. Each place had a paper napkin, a glass, and utensils. The clowns settled into their folding lawn chairs and started eating. It had already been a long day.

"A hundred and five," Wilhelmenia said.

"Wilhelmenia predicts a hundred and five," Ixnay said, writing the number next to her name in his notebook. It was a contest. The clowns always tried to guess the exact number of people who would show up for each performance. Ixnay was in charge of keeping the record. The winner got twenty dollars. If there was no winner, and there hardly ever was, the money got put into the party fund. Unless it was needed for food or some other shared expense.

"Fifty-nine," Guillermo said.

"Sixty-two," Lola said.

"Seventy-five," Wanda said.

"Forty-seven," Peppy said.

"Nine," Sweetpea said.

"Stop being an optimist," Henrietta said. The clowns got a laugh out of that one. Sweetpea shot her a look that could have knocked a rhinoceros out cold. Henrietta smiled. It was her main line of defense.

"Okay, ten," Sweetpea said.

"That's better," Henrietta said.

"Myself, I predict eighty-seven," Grandmother Spangle said.

"Two hundred and one," MoMo said.

"Pie in the sky," Guillermo said.

"Coconut cream pie in the sky," MoMo responded.

"Chocolate cream pie in the sky," Henrietta said.

"Ninety-seven," Grouchy said, wanting to get on with it.

Henrietta and MoMo grinned at each other.

"Apple pie in the sky," said father.

"Lemon pie in the sky," said daughter.

"Ninety-eight," Notz said.

"Ninety-nine," Ixnay said.

The Landorini brothers always chose three numbers in sequence.

"One hundred and seventy-five," Hortense said.

"Two hundred and fifty," Henrietta said. "Standing room only."

"We haven't had a full house in almost a year," Wilhelmenia said.

"We're going to have one tonight," Henrietta said.

After lunch, Ixnay backed the truck into the field. The clowns unloaded the ten racks of twenty-five seats, unfolded them, then bolted them together. The stage sections of wood flooring were set in place, fitted so they were seamless, then secured. Vertical lengths of iron pipe were fastened into weighted bases and joined together with a thin length of steel cable, which was then jacked tight. Curtain backdrops depicting barely discernible European country scenes were attached to the cable to form the stage's rear wall. There was no roof. When it rained, there was no show. The lights, sound system, smoke machine, and Wilhelmenia's electric calliope were all hooked to the big generator in back of Ixnay's truck. The clowns worked with practiced efficiency. Not a motion was wasted.

When they were done, they went off to rest, or to take care of personal business. Hortense said she was going to write her sister, to tell her when they were coming. MoMo pretended not to hear.

"The premise of the Eight-Foot-Tall is simple," he said to Henrietta when they were alone. "With you standing on my shoulders, minus the overlap of my head, we become one eight-foot-tall clown. Not two clowns pretending to be one, but to the eye of the audience the world's tallest clown, who can do astonishing things. The costume your mother is making will help the illusion, and I'll do my part, but most of all it will be up to you, dear girl. Balance, intuition, and trust."

"I trust you," Henrietta said.

"And I trust you," MoMo said. "It's trusting yourself I'm talking about."

MoMo leaned forward. Henrietta kicked off her flip-flops. She climbed quickly to her father's shoulders, then stood to her full height as MoMo straightened to his. It was a movement made in easy harmony. Henrietta had stood in her father's hand when she was hardly more than a baby. She'd stood on her father's head in one of their first routines together. She'd launched countless leaps into space from her father's shoulders. MoMo clasped his hands around his daughter's ankles and started walking about the stage.

"They'll see your face and arms and hands," MoMo said. "All they'll see of me is legs and feet. It's what you do up there that will sell the audience. If you do it right, they won't know there are two of us until the big reveal at the end."

"We'll knock their socks off," Henrietta said.

MoMo leaned to one side, then the other as he walked. He varied his speed. He stumbled intentionally. He changed directions abruptly. For a half hour they carried on this way, each playing his or her respective part of a single body.

Henrietta reveled in every minute of it.

MAKING UP

eppy made his specialty for dinner: peppers, onions, and fried salami. Henrietta cleaned up afterward, then put on her sneakers and ran three times around the perimeter of the field.

Her mother and father were arguing when she returned. She tried not to pay attention. One of the rules of living in a traveling clown circus was to walk away if you could, and close your ears if you couldn't. But this was her parents and she'd heard enough already to know that it involved her and she was already there by the steps, so she stayed. MoMo and Hortense seldom disagreed. When they did, they settled matters quickly. Henrietta couldn't remember hearing her mother so upset.

"I'm asking you to do this for me," Hortense said. "That should be enough."

"Why now all of a sudden?" MoMo asked in his most patient voice.

"It's not all of a sudden," she said. "I've been thinking about it for a while. It's important for her to meet Carlotta. And for Carlotta to meet her. Henrietta has to begin learning about life outside the circus. There are things she should know."

"She doesn't seem to be suffering that I can see," MoMo said. "And why are we fighting about something that isn't going to happen? Your sister won't let us in."

"If she doesn't, you have nothing to worry about," Hortense said. "Our daughter has to know that there's something else besides being a clown."

"There's nothing better than being a clown," MoMo shouted.

"What good is it if she can't make a living?" Hortense shouted back.

MoMo charged out the door in his baggy white pants with the red polka dots, suspenders over his undershirt, and long shoes that slapped the ground when he walked.

"I don't understand your mother sometimes," he said upon noticing Henrietta. He marched off waving his arms and yelling to himself about the futility of trying to comprehend the impossible.

A moment later Hortense appeared. "Sometimes I think we live in a dream," she said softly, almost as if to herself.

"Everything isn't Filbert's Traveling Clown Circus. There's a lot more to it than that. There's the rest of the world."

"I've never lived in the rest of the world," Henrietta said. "Anyway, what's wrong with this one?"

"Nothing," Hortense said, "but things change."

"They don't have to if we don't let them," Henrietta said.

"You are your father's daughter," Hortense said.

"I'm your daughter too," Henrietta said. "Why is he so mad about going to see Carlotta?"

"Because he tried to make peace with her after we got married. My sister wasn't nice about it. She called him an evil little man. She accused him of putting me under a spell. She said hurtful things. That was then. This is now. We're going to see her. We have to be prepared for what's next."

"What's next is tonight's show," Henrietta said. "We're going to do a lot of business on Long Island. We're going to be a big hit in Union Square."

"I hope so," Hortense said. "I have to test my equipment."

Henrietta watched her mother walk off. "I want things to stay the way they are," she said.

"So do I," Hortense said.

Henrietta went inside and stripped to her underwear. Things would get better soon, she thought. She stepped into her baggy white pants with the red polka dots. They were exactly like MoMo's. She snapped her suspenders into place. She slipped her feet into the long shoes that flapped on the ground when she walked and tied them tight. She sat on the bench at the dressing table and began painting on her white-face.

MoMo came in and sat beside her and painted on his whiteface, which was exactly the same as hers. They painted on red mouths. They attached red bulb noses. They stood and put on their baggy red shirts with the white polka dots. They pulled on frizzy wigs and hats and oversize gloves. They stood and inspected each other.

"We're the Hornbuckles," MoMo said to his daughter. "There are three of us. Always three."

THE SHOW

Wilhelmenia played her electric calliope, which to Henrietta always sounded like a herd of wild horses singing, if horses could sing. She was bathed in the blue spotlight Grandmother Spangle had trained on her. Peppy and Wanda were selling tickets and programs. Guillermo and Lola were hawking small bags of salted peanuts and cold bottles of soda pop. Hortense was at the controls of the sound system. Backstage, Henrietta and MoMo were checking their props. Ixnay, Grouchy, and Notz were lining up paper plates, which they'd fill later with whipped cream from cans for "Pie Time!"

Sweetpea observed with a bored expression from behind her makeup of sparkling freckles, orange hair with pigtails, and a straw hat. "Don't you ever get tired of this?" she asked, sidling up to Henrietta.

"Are you talking to me?" Henrietta asked. It had been

at least a week since Sweetpea had spoken to her directly.

"Not really," Sweetpea said. "Sometimes I think if I have to do this one more time I'll barf."

"Do what one more time?" Henrietta asked. She could see her father grinning.

"This," Sweetpea said. "Be a clown."

"How can you not want to be a clown?" To Henrietta the idea was preposterous.

"It's mindless," Sweetpea said.

"I love being a clown," Henrietta said, throwing her arms out wide at her sides, smiling her biggest theatrical smile. "There's nothing like it."

"That proves my point," Sweetpea said.

"What point?"

"If you love being a clown, it must be mindless."

Henrietta wasn't insulted. She didn't take most things personally. Besides, she didn't believe Sweetpea.

"What would you do instead?" she asked.

"Be normal," Sweetpea said. "Have an address."

"I'll always be a clown," Henrietta said.

"Not in this circus," Sweetpea said.

"There's nothing wrong with this circus."

Sweetpea dismissed her with a smile that suggested she was an idiot, then wandered off.

"Why does she say stuff like that?" Henrietta asked her father.

"It's her sense of humor," MoMo said.

The electric calliope went quiet. Hortense started the recorded music, which began with a long drumroll, followed by a fanfare of trumpets.

"Ladies and gentlemen," she announced into the microphone in front of her, "and all you splendid boys and girls. Welcome to Filbert's Traveling Clown Circus."

Henrietta loved hearing her mother announce the acts. She created the prospect of drama and excitement. She offered the promise of something wonderful.

"Tonight," Hortense continued, "thirteen of the most talented clowns on earth will entertain and delight you."

Laughter erupted from the sound system as Hortense played a tape that contained assorted giggles, guffaws, and belly laughs. Pretty quickly the audience was laughing along. Henrietta loved the sound of the real thing.

"And now," Hortense intoned, "to begin the night on the highest note possible, the legendary Wilhelmenia will perform her unique interpretation of the classical ballet *Swan Lake*."

Grandmother Spangle made adjustments on her control board. The stage lights came up slowly. A dense white cloud billowed forth from the smoke machine, which was operated by a Landorini brother. Hortense started the music. Wilhelmenia, all six feet four inches, two hundred and sixty-five pounds of her, emerged from the drifting cloud in a screaming red tutu and a football helmet with flowers growing out of it, riding on roller skates. Her appearance produced a moment of stunned silence, then laughter and applause.

Wilhelmenia skated gracefully, then with comic clumsiness. She performed intricate patterns. She tripped and stumbled and was constantly on the verge of losing control, which she never did. She skated off on one leg to cheering and applause.

The stage went dark. Hortense told their Greenport audience how hard it was for some people to get up in the morning and get ready for the day. Henrietta and MoMo carried their table to the center of the stage and set it down. They moved to opposite sides of the table's center and faced each other through the large empty picture frame that was secured to it. This created the illusion of a mirror, into which one of them stared and the other was the reflected image.

"And now," Hortense concluded, "the father-and-daughter team of MoMo and Henrietta performing their acclaimed mirror act."

An alarm clock rang. A large yellow spotlight became the early morning sun. MoMo and Henrietta stretched and yawned in perfect unison, mirror images of each other. They moved with such precision that there seemed to be only one of them.

They scratched their noses.

They scratched their rear ends.

They stifled a sneeze.

They sneezed.

What Henrietta did, MoMo did with the opposite hand,

or the opposite side of his face, or body. They knew each other's moves so well, either could follow the other or lead.

They lifted huge toothbrushes and worked them back and forth. They washed their faces. They shaved with huge, floppy rubber razors. They put on five-foot-long neckties. They took a moment to admire the result, then, at precisely the same moment, turned and walked off the stage in opposite directions.

The audience burst into applause. MoMo and Henrietta returned for their bow.

"The best father-and-daughter clown act anywhere," Hortense exclaimed.

Ixnay, Grouchy, and Notz performed their tumbling act, which consisted of them knocking one another over and constantly not catching one another until the end, when they did it perfectly.

Lola and Guillermo performed their magic. They kept making each other disappear. They danced a few tango steps, then disappeared together in a puff of smoke, followed by darkness.

Grandmother Spangle, Sweetpea, Ixnay, Notz, and MoMo did a clown version of "Little Red Riding Hood," in which the three bears showed up instead of the big bad wolf.

Peppy and Wanda juggled pillows, balloons, and scarves and an assortment of other difficult objects. Before Wanda was going to have the baby, they'd juggled nasty-looking knives. They could juggle almost anything.

Hortense dazzled as Cinderella. MoMo saved the day as the handsome prince. Henrietta, his trusted vassal, carried the glass slipper. Which was three feet long.

"It fits!" Hortense screamed ecstatically. She lifted MoMo into the air and kissed him.

Then Sweetpea, Grouchy, Lola, Henrietta, and Peppy did a routine on unicycles, joining hands finally and riding straight at the audience, stopping on a dime at the edge of the stage.

Grandmother Spangle lit up the big spot that created a circle of white light on the dark stage. A large ball appeared. It began rolling about. The spotlight followed. The ball moved in circles, then figure eights, then it zigged and zagged about as though alive. It began bouncing, higher and higher until it looked like it might fly away. Then it settled and finally came to a stop. The lights dimmed. A light came on inside the ball, revealing a figure. The ball separated into two halves, and MoMo jumped out.

Henrietta applauded harder than anyone. Someday she hoped to do what her father did inside that ball. He said he'd teach her when she was older and strong enough.

The stage went dark again. Ixnay, Grouchy, and Notz pushed the table of whipped cream pies to the center. All the clowns lined up, except Hortense, who handled sound and lights for this act. They moved past the table like it was a buffet, taking two pies each. They formed two lines that faced each other.

"Ladies and gentlemen, boys and girls," Hortense announced with glee in her voice, "it's 'Pie Time!'"

The clowns began hitting one another in the face with pies. Wham! Wham! Wham! Wham! Henrietta got Sweetpea, who got her back. MoMo got Wilhelmenia and Grouchy. Grouchy got Notz and Ixnay, who then got each other. Lola got Wanda, who got Peppy, who brought his pies together on each side of Guillermo's head, like they were cymbals. Grandmother Spangle, who'd been playing it tricky, snuck up on MoMo and got him square on. The clowns reloaded. Pies flew until they were gone. The stage went dark. Whipped cream was hastily wiped away.

28

"Ladies and gentlemen, and all you exceptional children who have graced us with your presence tonight, we of Filbert's Traveling Clown Circus thank you from the bottoms of our hearts," Hortense announced. "And now, our special good night to you."

Wilhelmenia began playing "Happy Days Are Here Again" on her electric calliope. MoMo moved into the spotlight and started singing in his strong baritone. Henrietta stepped into the light and added her sweet, clear soprano. Hortense was next. Her voice soared like a bird's. The Hornbuckles sang together, then the rest of the clowns joined in as Wilhelmenia picked up the tempo and the song became a celebration. After that they went around thanking all two hundred and fifty people who'd come to see them perform.

INTO THE NIGHT

oMo pinched his nostrils together between his thumb and forefinger and bleated out the tune to "Reveille," sounding as much like a bugle as he could. He did that directly into Henrietta's left ear.

Henrietta's eyes shot open.

"Rise and shine, dear girl," MoMo said.

Henrietta stretched. Her legs ached. She thought they must have cramped during the night.

"You are the clown of the hour," MoMo said. "You are our hero."

"It was a full house," Henrietta said, grinning.

"Standing room only," MoMo said.

"We're going to be all right now," Henrietta said.

"We're always going to be all right," MoMo said. He headed for the door. "There is work to be done and there are hearts to be won."

"I'm coming," Henrietta said. But not right away, she decided. She closed her eyes so she could better remember the night before.

After the show, after Wilhelmenia had tallied the take and deducted expenses, she'd handed out the remaining funds to each clown equally. That's how Filbert had run things, it was how she ran them still.

"We have a winner tonight," she'd said when business was concluded. "Henrietta predicted two hundred and fifty, and two hundred and fifty appeared." She'd handed her two crisp ten-dollar bills.

Henrietta had acknowledged the whistles and cheers. She'd climbed onto a chair and raised her glass of lemonade. It was a tradition that the winner say a few words.

"To Filbert's Traveling Clown Circus going on forever," she'd said, keeping it short so it would stick in everybody's mind.

"To Filbert's!" the clowns had all yelled back.

Henrietta opened her eyes, stretched again, then retrieved her prize money from beneath her pillow. She was going to save it for something special. She washed up, then dressed in orange and green shorts, a blue and white T-shirt, and flip-flops. She fortified herself with two fried egg sandwiches and two glasses of orange juice, then joined Sweetpea in walking the field, clearing it of empty soda cans and crumpled peanut bags.

"What do you want more than anything?" Sweetpea asked when they'd been at it awhile.

"You're talking to me again," Henrietta said, trying to sound shocked. "That's two days in a row."

"Just answer the question."

Henrietta wanted a lot of things. She wanted the circus to make money. She wanted to become a better clown. She wanted the Eight-Foot-Tall to be a big hit. She wanted to work with her mother and father forever.

"I want things to stay the same," she said.

"They can't," Sweetpea said. "It's circumstances."

"What circumstances?"

"Our circumstances."

"I don't know why you bother to talk to me," Henrietta said. "You never say anything I understand."

"What I want more than anything," Sweetpea said, "is a boyfriend."

"Why?"

"Because I've never had one," she said. She sighed loudly. "You're too young to understand."

They crisscrossed the field until it had been restored to its pristine state.

Lola, Wanda, and Notz spent the morning patching backdrop curtains and repairing costumes on the sewing machines the circus carried.

Hortense and Grandmother Spangle inspected wires and connections for the lights and sound system.

Peppy, Guillermo, and Ixnay checked engine fluids, tire pressures, fan belts, and hoses in all the vehicles.

Grouchy went into town looking for a grocery store that would make him a deal on a couple of cases of whipped cream.

MoMo and Wilhelmenia sat beneath the awning that pulled out from her RV, talking quietly about the immediate future.

At lunch, which was cheese sandwiches and tomato soup, everybody predicted a large turnout for the coming night's performance. They left it to Henrietta to choose another full house.

On their way to the next stop, which was west of Port Jefferson, MoMo rode in the truck with Ixnay because Hortense was giving Sweetpea a driving lesson. Henrietta rode in back of Wilhelmenia's RV with Grandmother Spangle, who was her teacher of thinking and listening. That's what Grandmother Spangle called it. Class was in session. Lately they'd been working on trying to put yourself in somebody else's shoes, which was called empathy.

Henrietta liked the time she spent with her teachers. Grouchy and Notz taught her history. Ixnay taught her how to repair and maintain engines. Lola and Guillermo taught her dancing and world culture. Wilhelmenia taught her math and bookkeeping. Peppy and Wanda taught her Spanish, cooking, and geography. Her mother taught her about books and art and music and writing. Her father taught her the craft of being a clown, and about life and living. MoMo set the example to which Henrietta aspired. Some of her lessons were taken with Sweetpea, but most she took alone. She revolved among her classes as she and her teachers felt like it, but she had at least one class almost every day of the year.

That afternoon Henrietta and MoMo rehearsed the Eight-Foot-Tall. Henrietta fell off her father's shoulders twice, both times landing on her feet and climbing quickly back on.

"It won't happen again," she said.

"Fall all you want while we're working on it," MoMo said.

"I don't like to fall," Henrietta said.

"Stop thinking about it," MoMo said. "Trust yourself. It will come together on opening night. You'll see." He started running around the stage like a drunk in a hurry.

Henrietta felt them spinning, then leaning until she was certain they'd topple over. She felt them pull back until they were standing straight and tall. MoMo's strength and agility freed Henrietta to concentrate on becoming the upper half of their body.

❂ ❂ ❂

That night fifty-one customers watched the show. The heat and humidity were in the low nineties. Costumes stuck to flesh. Makeup dribbled down faces. Whipped cream turned to paste. It wasn't any cooler when it came time to break down and stow the equipment.

"Our mother used to make us dunk our underwear in

water and put it in the freezer when we complained about it getting this hot," Notz said. "Right next to the ice cubes."

"She'd wait until they were stiff as boards, then make us put them on," Grouchy said.

34

"Try sticking your legs into a freezing cold pair of stuck-together, hard-as-rocks underwear sometime," Notz said.

"You're the one who complained," Ixnay said. "She did it because of you."

"I was eight years old," Notz said. "What did I know?"

"Cooled me off in a big hurry," Grouchy said.

"After you got over the shock," Ixnay said. "To this day I can't wear cold shorts."

This was all for Henrietta's benefit. She was helping the brothers pack the folding seat sections.

"My favorite part," Grouchy said, "was when my underwear started to melt and cold water ran down my legs. Better than air-conditioning."

"You're weird," Notz said.

Grouchy laughed. "Look who's talking."

A fork of lightning ripped through the dead-still air. Thunder erupted almost directly above them, an enormous blast that exploded without warning. It shook the ground. Henrietta sniffed at the sharp odor of ozone. The clowns picked up their pace.

"We've had worse nights than this," Henrietta said, referring to the weather and the poor turnout.

"Lots of them," MoMo said, climbing up into the back of the truck. He secured a tarpaulin over the generator.

Claps of thunder banged around them as they hurried to finish. Lightning seared the field across the road. Sheets of rain swept down on them, and the wind kicked into a fury as they got the last of their gear locked down.

"I'm going to check on Wanda," Hortense yelled.

Henrietta watched her mother until she was inside Wanda's RV, then went inside her own. MoMo started their small generator, which coughed, then caught. Henrietta turned on the light. MoMo put a kettle of water on the propane stove, then took down a jar of instant coffee. The RV rocked as it was hit by a hard gust of wind. Rain hammered the roof.

"You hungry?" MoMo asked.

Henrietta looked to see what there was to eat, and how much of it was left. The meals the clowns ate together were paid for by the circus's general expense fund. Their personal supplies came out of their own pockets. She took inventory: a box of wheat flakes, powdered milk, tea bags, a can of tomato sauce, half a jar of peanut butter, half a box of crackers, and a dented can of chicken noodle soup. She stood on her toes and pulled down the wheat flakes, then the powdered milk.

"How do you think we're doing with the Eight-Foot-Tall?" MoMo asked.

"We'll be one big clown by the time we're done," Henrietta said. "We'll be amazing."

"I want you to take chances up there," MoMo said. "Big gestures. Big emotions. Make them laugh. Make them gasp. You're who they're looking at."

36

Henrietta wasn't worried about the new routine. As with the others her father had taught her, they'd master this one. There wasn't anything they couldn't do together. Henrietta had other concerns.

"I don't want the circus to close," she said.

"Who said we're closing?" MoMo set his mug of coffee on the table, then pulled out the small trunk from the corner, opened it, and sat.

Henrietta mixed powdered milk with water and poured it over her wheat flakes. She moved a chair so she could be closer to her father. The trunk contained MoMo's old costumes. With each there was a story. She'd heard many of them, but not all.

"I was a mime before I was a clown," MoMo said.

A new story. Henrietta chewed on her cereal and waited.

"I had to make some money," MoMo said. "I'd seen mimes on the street. I studied them until I could do it myself."

"Mimes act out things without talking," Henrietta said.

"A big favorite was following somebody who walked by and mimicking everything they did. There weren't any other dwarf mimes around at the time, so I did okay. I was a novelty."

"How old were you?"

"Fourteen," her father answered.

"What did your mother and father say? Did they just let you go off? Did you have to sneak away?" Henrietta didn't know much about her grandparents because MoMo hadn't known his parents all that well himself. They'd been older when they adopted him, too old to be around when Henrietta came along.

"They were happy I'd found something to do," MoMo said. "They were afraid I wouldn't be able to take care of myself. When I told them I wanted to be a clown, they gave me their blessing and enough money to get by for six months."

"How could they let you leave when you were so young?"

"I was sixteen by then. They knew I could take care of myself. They knew I was leaving anyway."

"How long did it take you to become a clown?" Henrietta already knew the answer to this one. Some stories she never tired of hearing.

"I started almost right away," MoMo said. "I read books about clowns. I went to as many different circuses as I could. I experimented with what kind of face I wanted. I tried out different costumes. I rehearsed bits and routines over and over until I could do them in my sleep. Then I started working birthday parties and handing out promotions at gas stations and malls. I worked the kiddie sections of a couple of restaurants. Then I hooked up with a one-ring circus."

The door flew open, and Hortense blew in with the wind. She needed help getting the door closed behind her. She said she was spending the night with Wanda. The baby could come at any time.

"Tell Peppy he can sleep here if he wants to," MoMo said.

"He won't let go of her hand," Hortense said. She gathered a few of her things, kissed her husband and daughter, then battled her way back outside.

"Do you still have the mime costume?" Henrietta asked when she and her father were alone again.

"Just this," MoMo said, carefully removing a long-sleeve black T-shirt from the trunk. It was faded nearly to gray.

Henrietta examined it carefully. "Were you afraid of being on your own?"

"Sometimes," MoMo said. "I had to grow up fast."

"I'd be afraid," Henrietta said.

"You'd be all right," MoMo said. "You know how to look something in the eye and take care of it. Tomorrow we're switching the mirror act."

"I'm not as good doing it backward as you," Henrietta protested.

MoMo laughed. "That's what you always say."

They used the bathroom in turn, then went to bed. "I'd like to meet Carlotta," Henrietta said, tucking the two ten-dollar bills under her pillow.

"And why would that be?" her father asked from the bedroom.

"I want to see for myself."

"See what?"

"What she's like. Maybe she's changed."

"And maybe I'll play professional basketball when I'm too old to be a clown," MoMo said. "Let's talk about something pleasant, like Wanda and Peppy's baby."

"The first one born into the circus since me," Henrietta said.

"You'll keep an eye on the new clown," MoMo said. "Be the big sister."

"I will," Henrietta said. She was looking forward to it.

"Happy dreams, dear girl," MoMo said.

"Happy dreams, Pop," Henrietta said. She lay there listening to the distant rumble of thunder as the storm moved off. The rain had slackened. Tomorrow the sun would shine. More people would come.

UNEXPECTED DEVELOPMENTS

enrietta slept restlessly, turning and twisting and twitching as though having a bad dream. But she wasn't dreaming. Her body was being cranky. Her arm and leg joints ached, like they were being pulled at. She was startled awake by the cries of a newborn baby. She saw her father hopping out of the bedroom, pulling up his pants. She jumped into a pair of shorts, pulled on a T-shirt, and ran after him.

They gathered outside Peppy and Wanda's RV. Henrietta and MoMo and Sweetpea and Guillermo and Ixnay and Grouchy and Notz. The crying stopped. The door opened. Hortense stepped out and took a deep breath. Lola, Wilhelmenia, and Grandmother Spangle emerged after her.

"Everybody okay?" MoMo asked.

"Baby Boris made his appearance at roughly seven pounds just a short while ago," Hortense said.

"Wanda is feeling fine," Lola said.

"How's Peppy?" Guillermo asked.

"Close to passing out he's so happy," Grandmother Spangle said.

"We're fourteen clowns now," Henrietta said. "If we had more babies, we could become a big circus."

"One will do for the moment," Wilhelmenia said.

The women went back inside to help Wanda. The men yelled their congratulations, then returned to their RVs.

Henrietta stayed behind. She was thinking about the idea of a new life, and how good it made her feel to be part of it, even if she'd been told there were already too many people in the RV to let her witness the birth.

"Maybe Boris won't want to be a clown," Sweetpea said. She'd stayed as well.

"Maybe he'll be the greatest clown who ever lived," Henrietta replied.

"I wish I'd seen him being born," Sweetpea said.

"Me too," Henrietta said.

"You're too young," Sweetpea said, heading to her RV.

"I am not!" Henrietta yelled.

She fell asleep that night trying to decide what she'd teach Boris first. She and MoMo had worked together before she was a year old. The three Hornbuckles did their first routine when she was fourteen months. She wanted to do something original with Boris, so it could be just theirs.

❂   ❂   ❂

Henrietta went to meet the new arrival before breakfast. The sun was bright in a bottomless blue sky. The air felt like it had been scrubbed clean. She waited patiently for Wilhelmenia, who'd been in there far too long. Henrietta was eager to introduce herself. She wanted to tell Boris she'd be looking out for him. She figured it wasn't too early to start. Wilhelmenia filled the doorway.

42

"Not now," she said.

"Is something wrong?" Henrietta asked.

"After the meeting."

"What meeting?"

"The one we're about to have," Wilhelmenia said. She clapped her hands and yelled for everybody to come. The clowns gathered quickly.

"Peppy has something to say," she announced.

Peppy appeared from his RV. He grinned at the cheers that greeted him, then got serious. "This is the hardest thing I've ever had to do in my life," he said. "Wanda and I decided this morning that we're going home. Looking after Boris made us realize we have to change how we do things."

"*This* is home," Henrietta said, trying to sort out what was happening. Were they leaving for good? How could that be possible?

"We have family outside Denver," Peppy said. "We're going to live with them until we can get something of our own."

"You have a job lined up?" MoMo asked.

"Wanda has an uncle in the construction business," Peppy said. "There's always been a job waiting for me."

"Why can't you stay?" Henrietta asked. "Boris will be a great clown." She felt her father's hand pressing on her shoulder.

"We're free people," MoMo said quietly. "No notice is required to leave. There are no hard feelings."

"But they can't just go," Henrietta protested. It had never happened before. Nobody had left the circus since she was born.

"They can," MoMo said, "and we'll wish them well."

Henrietta knew there was nothing she could do to change the outcome. She could tell that from her father's sad smile, and from the way the others seemed willing to accept what was happening. She was glad she didn't have a family waiting outside the circus to claim her, or a job waiting, or anyplace to go other than where she was.

"We should give them what's in the party fund," Hortense said. "For Boris and the trip."

"Second the motion," Lola said.

"All in favor?" Wilhelmenia asked.

They voted yes. The fund would produce one hundred and eighty dollars, a meager amount given what lay ahead. It was a long way to Denver.

Peppy invited them to meet Boris before they left.

Henrietta decided she didn't want to. Why bother? She'd never see him again. She wasn't going to be his big sister.

She stewed on it for a while, then changed her mind. MoMo had said to wish them well.

Boris was sleeping when it was Henrietta's turn. She studied the tiny face, which was splotchy and scrunched up into a serious expression that made him look worried. The baby had a thatch of dark hair.

44

"We're going to miss you," Wanda said. She was on the couch holding her son.

Henrietta wanted to tell her not to go. "I'm going to miss you," she said instead.

"We've known you all your life," Wanda said. "We helped you grow up. It's sad to leave, but we have to."

"We're going to start doing better," Henrietta said, unable to stop herself from one last try. "You could stay awhile and see what happens. Maybe you wouldn't have to go."

"It's not like it was when you were born," Wanda said. "The circus had a future then. Boris has to lead a different life than this."

"I came to wish you well," Henrietta said, not wanting to prolong the agony. She was accepting something she didn't want because her father had told her it was how they did things. She didn't have to like it.

"We wish you well," Wanda said. "However things work out."

"I'll always be a clown," Henrietta said. She reached into her pocket, found the two ten-dollar bills, and handed them to Wanda.

"For when Boris needs something," she said. She leaned in and kissed Wanda, then the baby.

Wanda started crying.

Henrietta took a last look at Boris, silently wishing him good luck, then went to find Peppy.

"Don't give up," Peppy said, giving her a hug.

"Never," Henrietta said.

45

❖ ❖ ❖

The clowns watched Peppy and Wanda's RV drive off, bouncing erratically as it went. An hour later the remainder of the caravan headed for an area on the other side of Smithtown. Henrietta's lessons were canceled for the day.

It had all happened so fast, Henrietta thought. How was it possible to be with people your whole life, then suddenly not have them there at all? It occurred to her that everybody in the circus had come from someplace else, even Sweetpea, who'd been born in Pittsburgh and hadn't joined Filbert's until she was two, when she'd come with Grandmother Spangle to be with Wilhelmenia. With Boris gone, Henrietta was still the only one born to it.

"I don't understand why they couldn't stay," she said.

"A circus is no place to raise a child," her mother said.

"There's nothing wrong with me," Henrietta said.

"I'm not saying there is," Hortense said.

"Then there's nothing wrong with being raised in a circus," Henrietta said. "Look how I turned out."

"A gem among gems," her father said.

"Boris would have learned a lot more if he'd stayed," Henrietta said. "More than he'll learn in school."

"You've had a great education," MoMo said.

"We're concerned about what you're going to do when you get older," Hortense said.

"Be a clown," Henrietta said. "A clown can always make a living."

"Tell her," Hortense said.

"Tell me what?" Henrietta asked when MoMo didn't say anything.

"We have to start thinking about the future," MoMo said, sounding uncomfortable.

"Day to day," Henrietta said, "that's how we live."

"If we stayed in one place you could go to school," Hortense said. "Contrary to what you might think, there are a few things you don't know."

"The circus keeps moving," Henrietta said. "I can learn what I need right here."

"Nevertheless, we have to be ready," Hortense said.

"This is where I live," Henrietta said. "You're here. My friends are here. Why can't it just stay that way?"

"Because sometimes there's no choice," her mother said.

"We don't have to stop being a circus," Henrietta said.

"Can we talk about this later?" MoMo asked.

"You agreed we'd deal with it together," Hortense said.

"We will," MoMo said. "But not right now. Not all at once."

"The circus can keep going no matter what," Henrietta said, hammering down the nail on the subject as hard as she could.

"I've decided to go with you when you visit your sister," MoMo said.

Hortense gave her husband a suspicious look.

"I could use a little excitement," MoMo said. He grinned. "Besides, I've been outvoted, two to one. Your daughter supports you. Who am I to stand in the way?"

"You'll behave?"

"We will be at our winning best, won't we, dear girl?"

"We will," Henrietta said.

"Thank you," Hortense said.

Henrietta thought about her mother's increasing interest in the future. Hortense thought the circus was going to close, but she was wrong. Henrietta was sure she'd change her mind. Things had to improve. They always had gotten better after they'd been worse. Why should now be any different? Tomorrow would always become today. Today the circus was alive.

She heard her parents laughing. They were recalling some of the good times they'd had with Peppy and Wanda. She found herself feeling better.

THE SHOW GOES ON

MoMo made his way around the stage. Henrietta rode on his shoulders. They were rehearsing the Eight-Foot-Tall. MoMo stopped suddenly and bent down on one knee.

"Tie your shoe," he said.

Henrietta leaned forward and down until she reached her father's foot. She went through the exaggerated motions of knotting the laces.

"Your mother wants me to talk to you," MoMo said. "The future is coming whether we like it or not."

Henrietta straightened as her father stood. "So what if it's coming? It's not here yet."

MoMo started doing the leg part of jumping jacks. Henrietta did the arms. They didn't miss a beat.

"We have to be ready," MoMo said.

"Ready for what?"

"For whatever comes along."

"What if nothing comes along?"

"Believe me," MoMo said, "something always does."

"Like what?"

"It's hard to know. Nobody can predict what's going to happen next."

"Then why bother?" Henrietta asked. "If we don't know what it is, how can we get ready? What if we get ready for the wrong thing? What if it turns out there's nothing to get ready for? Why can't we forget about the future until it gets here and we see what it is?"

"Your mother is looking ahead in a practical way," MoMo said. "She wants to make sure you'll be okay when the time comes."

From jumping jacks they went on to moves they'd rehearsed earlier. Henrietta could picture the sequence that was being put together. MoMo's shifts of weight were becoming her own.

"She wants you to have something else to trade on," MoMo said.

"You don't have something else to trade on," Henrietta said.

"Being a clown might not always pay the rent," MoMo said.

"We don't pay rent," Henrietta said. "I don't think we should talk about the future anymore."

"It's something we have to think about," MoMo said. "Your mother is right about that."

"Maybe after she's seen Carlotta she'll remember why she became a clown and that will be the end of it," Henrietta said.

"I was something besides a clown once," MoMo said.

"You never told me that before," Henrietta said.

"I was with a circus that closed down in Lincoln, Nebraska."

"What happened? What did you do?"

MoMo pitched himself forward, and Henrietta tucked her head and rolled. MoMo rolled after her, and they crossed the stage like a runaway wheel.

"I started hitchhiking my way east," MoMo said. "I did odd jobs for food and a place to sleep and sometimes a little money. One night I had a couple of extra bucks and went to see some touring professional wrestlers. Afterward I found the boss and told him he could use a dwarf. I did some tumbling, showed him how strong I was, and he hired me."

"You were a professional wrestler?" Henrietta thought this had to be the most extraordinary thing her father had ever revealed.

They came out of the wheel maneuver, and MoMo started dancing. "I worked with a giant named Edgar. All four hundred pounds of him. Slow as a boulder. Sweet guy. We were billed as David and Goliath. The comic relief. I'd run around in between his legs and bother him the way a mosquito bothers an elephant. Once in a while he'd pick me up and throw me across the ring. I'd land like I was hurt. I'd stagger around, and he'd get ready to put me away when I'd kick his feet out from under him. He'd fall like a redwood. He was a great faller, Edgar. I always won. That was the joke."

"How'd you get to be a clown again?" Henrietta was trying to picture her father in the ring with a giant.

51

"Gentle as he was, Edgar would forget sometimes how big he was, and how small I was, and he'd sit on me. It was only a matter of time before he flattened me beyond repair. I tried talking him into becoming a clown. He tried talking me into staying a wrestler. We said goodbye in Terre Haute, Indiana. I hooked up with a small circus passing through."

"I'm going to stay a clown," Henrietta said after thinking about it for a minute.

❖ ❖ ❖

The fading sunset was a wide brushstroke of muted pink and yellow wash across the darkening sky. The company of Filbert's took this to be a good sign. Wilhelmenia began playing her electric calliope. Sweetpea and Notz sold tickets and programs. Lola and Guillermo sold cold soda and salty peanuts. Hortense and Grandmother Spangle were at their stations. Henrietta and MoMo checked their props. Ixnay and Grouchy lined up paper plates in preparation for "Pie Time!"

"Ladies and gentlemen," Hortense announced, which was followed by an enormous *pop*, followed by a series of snaps and crackles. A geyser of sparks shot into the air from the back of Ixnay's truck. The generator cut out. The calliope went silent. The circus fell into darkness.

"Make an announcement," Wilhelmenia ordered as she rushed backstage in her tutu and football helmet and roller skates. "You!" She pointed at Henrietta. "Tell them we'll get started in a few minutes. Entertain them. The rest of you get your RV generators going." She headed for the truck. Ixnay was already there.

"What should I do?" Henrietta asked her father. She'd never played this role before.

"Enjoy yourself," MoMo said. He handed his daughter a flashlight and took off after the others. They'd unhook the connections to the big generator and redistribute them to the small generators. It was tricky, but they'd had practice.

Henrietta stepped out onto the stage and made her way in the darkness to its front edge. She could discern the crowd and hear their growing impatience. She positioned the flashlight under her chin.

"Good evening!" she shouted, turning the light on at the same moment. Her face appeared in the upward beam, making it seem like a disembodied head.

"Ladies and gentlemen and excellent children," she continued, trying to sound as much like her mother as she could, "the show will begin in just a minute."

"What happened to the lights?" somebody shouted from the seats.

"The bulb blew out," Henrietta said. "Who knows how many clowns it takes to change a lightbulb?" It was a joke she'd heard MoMo tell. She was showered with numbers from the audience.

"It takes twenty-two clowns to change a lightbulb," Henrietta said. "One to hold the bulb, one to turn the clown holding the bulb, and twenty to throw the pies." It got a few laughs. Not as many as she'd hoped for.

Because she couldn't do anything physical in the dark, she started singing, "Let a Smile Be Your Umbrella." The audience quieted down. A few moments later a spotlight sprang to life and encircled her. Her mother's voice filled the air, asking everybody to give Henrietta Hornbuckle a big hand. She bowed and ran off. Hortense announced Wilhelmenia and *Swan Lake*. Henrietta felt her father's hand on her shoulder.

"Well done, dear girl," MoMo said.

Despite being one act short and having the generator break down, the show went off without a hitch.

FILBERT'S TAKES A HOLIDAY

The caravan passed through the town of Huntington. Calliope music blasted. Grandmother Spangle announced the time and place of the show. Henrietta, MoMo, Sweetpea, Lola, and Notz rode unicycles down the middle of the street, juggling balls and bowling pins and small hoops. They were greeted with smiles and waves of encouragement. Henrietta was sure they'd have a big audience for tonight's performance. Fewer than a hundred had showed up the night before.

They drove to the field they used each year and formed the RVs into a circle. A police car pulled in. The officer told them they had to leave. Their permit to use the field had been canceled.

Wilhelmenia produced her paperwork, including the letter from the owner giving them permission. The cop told her the property had been sold.

"Let me talk to the new owner," Wilhelmenia said. "I'm sure they'll let us stay when they know who we are."

"They know who you are," the cop said.

MoMo asked him for time to find another location. "Otherwise we'll have to cancel," he said.

"They don't want you here," the cop said.

"Why?" Henrietta demanded. "What's wrong with us?" She walked on her hands, sang a couple of lines of "Yankee Doodle Boy," then flipped to her feet. "We're here today, gone tomorrow. We're a circus."

The cop smiled. "I'm sorry. They don't seem to like clowns. It would be better if you just left. I don't want to make anything out of this."

"To the mall," Wilhelmenia ordered. "We'll figure it out from there."

As they drove away, Henrietta thought about all the times they'd been told to move on. "What kind of people don't like clowns?" she asked her parents.

"The kind who don't appreciate life," MoMo said. "They don't see that it can be funny and sad at the same time."

"Some people don't like the way we live," Hortense said. "They think there must be something wrong with us because we're always moving."

Henrietta knew there were people who thought they were thieves, or up to no good of some sort. She knew there were people who were frightened of clowns, or even thought them evil.

"Some think we're hiding something behind our makeup," MoMo said.

"Maybe they think those are our real faces we paint on," Henrietta said.

"There's no show tonight," MoMo said. "What can we do instead?"

Henrietta was hoping for a movie. They went a few times a year. She didn't care what they saw.

"We can do laundry," Hortense said.

"Ah, laundry," MoMo said. "Where would we be without it?"

"We're going to make ourselves presentable for Carlotta," Hortense said.

"What's wrong with the way I look?" Henrietta asked.

"Nothing," her mother said. "My sister won't be used to it, that's all."

Henrietta didn't understand the problem. She'd been picking out what she wore since she was old enough to dress herself. She liked checks and stripes and lots of colors, so long as nothing matched. Presently, she was wearing orange and blue shorts and a sleeveless black T-shirt with small green fish swimming on the front.

"Nobody ever complained about the way I dress before," she said.

"We'll do our laundry and present ourselves to Carlotta looking like nothing less than a million bucks each," MoMo said.

"That's exactly what we'll do," Henrietta said.

They followed Wilhelmenia to the parking lot of a cinder-block strip mall. A discount store where everything was five bucks or less, a Chinese restaurant, a hair salon and tanning studio, a video rental store, a resale clothing outlet, and a Laundromat were open for business. Three storefronts were for rent.

Industrial-size washers were stuffed full of clothes and costumes. Soap was poured. Handfuls of quarters set the machines in motion. Henrietta watched a pair of her underwear take center stage in the porthole. Next came one of her father's costumes. Then a pair of her mother's socks. Sweetpea plunked herself down in the next chair, but Henrietta paid no attention. She was thinking about Wanda and Peppy and Boris, about how far they'd gotten, and if they were all right.

"I could steal your clothes and you wouldn't even know it," Sweetpea said. "That's how out of it you are."

"Why would you steal my clothes?"

"I wouldn't," she said, "but I could. You have to pay attention in the real world."

"Go ahead and steal them if it makes you happy."

"You could make a person crazy," Sweetpea said.

They'd been left to guard the laundry. The rest of the clowns had gone off to do errands. They didn't often get the chance.

"I'm going to have somebody wash my clothes for me

someday," Sweetpea said, unwrapping a candy bar. "I'm going to have somebody do my cooking and cleaning."

"Who's going to do that for you?" Henrietta eyed the stick of chocolate with nuts and caramel inside.

"My staff." Sweetpea broke off a piece of the candy. "My staff is going to do everything except what I want to do myself."

"Where are you going to get a staff?"

"I'm going to be rich," Sweetpea said. She handed Henrietta the piece she'd broken off.

Henrietta stared at it, wondering why all of a sudden Sweetpea would be willing to share something with her. She took a small bite. "How are you going to be rich?"

"I read magazines," Sweetpea said. "I read about rich people. They're not all smart. Some of them are flat-out stupid. If they can do it, I can do it."

"I don't want to be rich," Henrietta said.

"You like being poor?"

"Who's poor?"

"We are," Sweetpea said.

"We are not."

"Everything is falling apart," Sweetpea said. "The RVs. All the equipment. Even our costumes. There's no money to fix anything. There's hardly enough for food and gas."

"Ixnay keeps us going," Henrietta said.

"The circus is old and worn out," Sweetpea said.

"It is not." Henrietta was getting agitated. "You just don't like being a clown."

"You can deny it all you want," Sweetpea said, "but all you have to do is look to know I'm telling the truth."

"We're not poor," Henrietta yelled, drawing glances from the Laundromat's other patrons. She didn't care. There wasn't anything she wanted that she didn't already have. She thought of giving Sweetpea back the remainder of the candy, then ate it.

"Nobody gets paid," Sweetpea said, "unless we have a big night, and we hardly ever have those anymore."

"Even if it's true," Henrietta said, "even if everything is old and worn out, it doesn't mean the circus can't keep going. We'll do better, then we'll have the money we need and we won't be poor anymore."

Sweetpea shook her head sadly. "You don't know anything," she said.

They moved the laundry into dryers, which they got spinning with more handfuls of quarters. Henrietta wondered why hot air cost so much.

Sweetpea attached her headphones to her ears and started reading a year-old fashion magazine she'd found buried beneath a stack of last week's newspapers.

Henrietta spent her time trying to imagine what it would be like if there were no circus and they lived in a house. She tried, but she couldn't. In a house you wouldn't be able to drive off when you wanted to be somewhere else. In a house you'd be stuck in the same place forever. She couldn't get past that.

Hortense and MoMo returned, then the others. Laundry was folded and put away. Henrietta went off with her mother to the resale clothing outlet.

"We don't carry kids' stuff," the owner said from behind his desk, which was on a raised platform in the middle of the store. His heavy-lidded eyes darted about, like he thought somebody might be sneaking up on him.

"You must have small sizes," Hortense said.

"Odd sizes over in that corner," the owner said, pointing. "Shirts, shoes, pants, jackets, dresses, big, small, whatever."

Hortense quickly found a brown cotton skirt she could alter to fit her daughter. None of the shoes fit, so sneakers would have to do. The rack holding shirts produced two candidates. Her mother favored the pale blue; Henrietta thought the burgundy with pearly buttons and a yellow butterfly stitched on its back was about the finest shirt she'd ever seen.

"It's too much like the shirts you already have," Hortense said.

"I don't have a butterfly."

"I don't want my sister looking at your shirt, I want her looking at you."

"It's got class," Henrietta said.

"That's your father talking," Hortense said.

"I'd feel good in a shirt like this," Henrietta said.

"I'd feel good with you in a plain blue shirt," Hortense said, holding it up. She could shorten the sleeves if she had time. Otherwise they could be rolled. "Sometimes we dress for the occasion. Sometimes pleasing others helps the cause. It doesn't mean anything more than that."

"I wouldn't be me," Henrietta said.

"Who would you be?"

"Somebody in a plain blue shirt."

"You'd be an aspect of yourself," Hortense said. "Think of it that way. You're a girl of many aspects."

"What aspect would I be in a plain blue shirt?"

"The less usual aspect," Hortense said. "The unexpected aspect. You could wear a shirt like this and not get stared at."

"I don't mind being stared at."

"I know you don't."

"If I don't grow taller, I'll get stared at for the rest of my life."

"You'll grow taller."

"Then I won't be able to do the Eight-Foot-Tall."

"All we're talking about here is a shirt," Hortense said.

"The one with the butterfly," MoMo said, sauntering up the aisle. He was swinging a beaded necklace on one finger. "It's got my girl's name written all over it. This is for you." He held up the necklace of amber glass and presented it to his wife.

"What's the occasion?" she asked.

"Today is the occasion," he said. "It's the most important day in human history."

"And why is that?" she asked.

"Because we're here," Henrietta said.

"Give that girl a prize from the top shelf," MoMo said. He kissed his wife. "It's also because you put up with me."

Hortense lowered her neck, and MoMo fastened the necklace around it.

"I made a deal with the owner," MoMo said. "I gave him three tickets for the Oyster Bay show and told him to bring his family backstage afterward. The clothes are on the house." The clowns traded tickets for things they needed whenever they could.

"I'll take the blue shirt," Henrietta said. She figured it meant more to her mother than it did to her. Besides, she could cut the collar and sleeves off later.

"Thank you," Hortense said to her husband and daughter. "Gifts from the loves of my life."

◈ ◈ ◈

Wilhelmenia said she was picking up the check for dinner. She wouldn't say why. They sat around the big table in the corner of the Chinese restaurant passing platters of noodles and shrimp and beef and a whole cooked fish and vegetables and heaps of rice. Henrietta ordered the boneless fried chicken because she'd never heard of such a thing.

"They raise them that way," Grouchy said.

"They do not," Henrietta said.

"I've seen them myself," Notz said. "There's a boneless chicken ranch in Tennessee."

"And I suppose they just flop around all day," Henrietta said.

"No way," Notz said. "They blow them up and float them."

"Fill them with helium," Grouchy said. "Tie strings to their legs so they won't get away."

Henrietta pictured chickens floating around like little feathered blimps. She laughed.

Wilhelmenia made her announcement while the fortune cookies were being opened. "I called the owner of the field in Oyster Bay. He said we can come early at no additional charge."

The clowns applauded the news. They had a place to spend the night. Oyster Bay was less than an hour's drive. They'd get a decent rest and have an entire day to set up.

Henrietta cracked open her fortune cookie. "A big surprise is right around the corner," she read. That had to mean Aunt Carlotta.

CARLOTTA

enrietta was awake and waiting when the first light of day crept in around the shades covering the RV's windows. Between speculating about her aunt and trying to ignore her aching arm and leg joints, she hadn't slept all that much. She peed, washed, brushed her teeth, and tied her hair into a ponytail with a green ribbon. She dressed in red and green striped shorts, a black and white T-shirt, and sneakers. She stepped outside, inhaled the freshness of the morning, then started running.

She was curious about her aunt. She was eager to meet her and anxious about it at the same time. She wanted her mother and her aunt to be friends because it would make her mother happy. If Henrietta got along with Carlotta, it might make things easier. But she had also come to understand that Carlotta figured in her mother's plans for the future some- how, and those she did not want to succeed at all.

She ran along a narrow road, past gated estates. She ran easily, hardly breaking a sweat. She saw horses being let out into a pasture, then two dogs chasing each other. She felt the *Whoooosh!* of a car's back draft as it came up behind her and sped by. She cut off onto another road that took her past large gnarled trees that may have been witness to the Revolutionary War, then ran on a street of modest houses. A mile later she was back at the caravan. The clowns were stirring. Hortense and MoMo sat in front of their RV sipping from mugs of coffee.

"Good morning, Henrietta Hornbuckle," Hortense said.

"Good morning, dear girl," MoMo said. "How about a dress rehearsal of the Eight-Foot-Tall later on? Your mother has finished the costume."

"We're seeing Carlotta today," Hortense said.

"We'll be ready," MoMo said.

The morning was devoted to setting up the seats and stage. Then Henrietta, Lola, Grouchy, Sweetpea, and Notz made their way through downtown Oyster Bay, followed by Wilhelmenia's RV, with its calliope music and Grandmother Spangle's announcements. They stopped at a park and put on a five-minute promotional show for about forty people, gave away a few tickets, and called it a day.

❂ ❂ ❂

After lunch, Henrietta and MoMo painted on their faces, then put on their costumes. She pulled on the long shirt of many colored vertical stripes that her mother had made. It was padded in the shoulders to make her look as wide as an eight-foot-tall clown might be. It tapered to her feet, where a belt had been sewn on to create the illusion of a waist. The oversize wig she pinned to her hair and the hat she pinned to her wig doubled the size of her head. MoMo put on pants of the same colored stripes as his daughter's shirt. They came to his neck and fastened with a drawstring, creating the illusion of long legs. A hole in Henrietta's fake belt buckle enabled MoMo to see where he was going.

Father and daughter checked each other over, then headed for the stage, looking like the top and bottom halves of a single person walking side by side.

Hortense started the music she'd selected. "Ladies and gentlemen," she announced to the clowns who'd gathered to watch, "for the first time anywhere, Filbert's Traveling Clown Circus is honored to present the Eight-Foot-Tall Clown."

MoMo sprang through the opening in the curtain with Henrietta riding on his shoulders. Their costume fit them perfectly. When they were standing still, you couldn't tell it was two people. But MoMo wasn't standing still. He was a man out of control. He stumbled, nearly fell, regained his balance, came within an inch of falling off the stage, veered sharply away at the last moment, then did a split. Henrietta shot her arms out at her sides.

They got better as they went. Bolder. More daring. They performed all that they'd rehearsed and a few moves they hadn't. Henrietta floated, as if she'd lost touch with gravity.

There was no universe, no planet earth, no circus. There was just her and her father, and they'd become a single person. Then she felt MoMo's signal, and she leapt into the air. Their costumes separated. Henrietta did three somersaults and came down on her feet next to her father.

"Ladies and gentlemen," Hortense shouted, "Henrietta and MoMo and the Eight-Foot-Tall Clown!"

"Your name is supposed to come first," Henrietta said.

"Not in this case, dear girl," MoMo said. "In this case you come first."

Then they were surrounded by the other clowns, who told them it was one of the greatest acts they'd ever seen. Wilhelmenia said it would go in whenever it was ready.

MoMo said they'd do it at Union Square.

Henrietta was sure they'd be much better by then.

Hortense said it was time to get ready for Carlotta. Father and daughter went to clean themselves up.

MoMo shaved and put on his best pants, a pullover shirt with a collar, and his moccasins, with socks.

"You look acceptable for tea," Hortense said after inspecting him.

"We're having tea?" Henrietta asked.

"If we have anything, it will be tea," her mother said. "If my sister lets us in, she'll be a proper host. She was always big on tea."

Hortense wore her best dress, which was pale yellow with red roses on it. She took out the necklace MoMo had given her. She lowered her head, and he fastened it around her neck. She applied her lipstick with great care.

Henrietta buttoned her blue shirt and tucked it into her brown skirt. She felt uncomfortable in her new clothes. She saw her father smiling.

"Something the matter with the way I look?" she asked.

"The opposite," he said. "You look divine."

"I'd rather talk about Aunt Carlotta," Henrietta said.

"My lips are sealed on the subject," MoMo said.

"Good," Hortense said.

"Then mine will be too," Henrietta said.

"Double good," her mother said. "Carlotta is five years older than I am. It's been thirteen years since we saw each other. I have no idea what she's like, or how she looks. We'll see for ourselves when we get there."

Henrietta could tell her mother was nervous.

"I'm keeping an open mind," MoMo said.

"Me too," Henrietta said.

"It's getting harder and harder to tell when you two are serious," Hortense said. "I'd appreciate your cooperation."

"You've got mine," MoMo said.

"Mine too," Henrietta said.

❂ ❂ ❂

They walked to Carlotta's. MoMo had wanted to drive. Hortense had made it clear that they weren't showing up at her sister's in their circus wagon. They'd gotten directions. It was half a mile. Hortense and MoMo held hands. Henrietta ran ahead to harvest a bunch of ragged blue and white prickly-stemmed flowers that were growing by the side of the road. She handed one to her mother.

"It's beautiful," Hortense said.

"The rest are for Carlotta," Henrietta said.

"You're a charmer," MoMo said.

"Why doesn't she like the circus?" Henrietta asked.

"Because she doesn't know how to have fun," MoMo said.

"No circus talk," Hortense said. "If she asks, talk about something else."

"I'm not ashamed of what I do," MoMo said.

"Neither am I," Hortense said, "but it will only make things more difficult."

Henrietta wondered what she'd talk about if she couldn't talk about the circus. She'd meant to convince her aunt that no life was better. When Carlotta saw how well she was doing, her mother and father would be forgiven for getting married and everybody would be happy. Then they'd do the show tonight and get moving.

"What an absolutely glorious day," MoMo exclaimed suddenly, like it was a major announcement. "There isn't a man on earth with my good fortune."

They left the country road and made their way along a street of substantial Victorian houses. The one that bore Carlotta's address was set behind a tall, neatly trimmed hedge. MoMo opened the iron gate, then followed his wife and daughter up the brick walk to the wide front porch. They stood at the door and collected themselves.

Henrietta realized that she was about to set foot inside a house for the first time. She peered through the door's cut-glass panels, but couldn't see anything except weird shapes and colors.

 70

"Here goes nothing," Hortense said. She took a deep breath, then released it slowly.

"Nobody can say you didn't try," MoMo said.

"If she doesn't want to see us, there's nothing I can do about it," Hortense said.

"Nothing," Henrietta said, eager to be inside. There would be rooms and stairs. She'd seen pictures. She had a general idea.

"It's not up to me," Hortense said.

"It's up to her," MoMo said.

"She's going to love us," Henrietta said.

Her mother reached to ring the bell.

The door opened before she got there.

"You are expected," a man who was plump as a marshmallow said. He inspected them with curiosity. His eyes were large and almond-shaped. He wore a white shirt and white trousers.

"I'm Fenimore," he said. "I'll show you to the library." He snatched the flowers from Henrietta's hand. "I'll put these in water. Madam will be pleased."

"They're for Carlotta," Henrietta said.

"Madam and Carlotta are one and the same," Fenimore said.

"Why is she madam if she's Carlotta?" Henrietta asked. She felt her mother's gentle poke, the signal to lay off.

"*Madam* is what the situation calls for," Fenimore said.

"What situation?" Henrietta asked, despite her mother's warning.

"The situation of my employment," Fenimore said.

They followed him past a staircase that ascended in two stages to the second floor. Henrietta was sure their RV would fit into the hall, with room left over to put out the lawn chairs. She eyed the portraits of people in old-fashioned clothes that lined both walls.

"Who are they?" she asked her mother.

"I have no idea," Hortense said.

"They look like a lot of well-dressed crooks," MoMo said.

Hortense poked him. Henrietta saw it and grinned. Fenimore stood aside, and they entered a room that was filled with more paintings of people in old-fashioned clothes, and large pieces of stiff-looking furniture. The fireplace was big enough for Henrietta to walk into. Shelves of books rose from floor to ceiling, which was capped with a stained-glass dome.

"How do you get the books off the top shelf?" Henrietta asked.

"The ladder," Fenimore said, directing her attention to it. There were rollers on the bottoms of its legs.

"Madam will be with you in a minute," Fenimore said, preparing to leave.

"What's she doing?" Henrietta asked, expecting another poke from her mother.

"Preparing," Fenimore said.

"For what?" Henrietta asked. The poke arrived.

"Never mind," Hortense said.

"She won't be long," Fenimore said, starting for the door.

"Where's the bathroom?" Henrietta asked.

"Directly across the hall," Fenimore said as he departed.

"Who is he?" Henrietta asked.

"The butler," Hortense answered.

"She must have won the lottery," MoMo said. He moved to a window and studied the yard.

"Something sure happened," Hortense said. She directed her attention to the books.

Henrietta checked up and down the hall, then darted into the room on the other side, turned on the light, and closed the door. It was the most remarkable bathroom she'd ever seen. The sink was made of black marble, as was the toilet. The fixtures looked like gold. The wallpaper showed people on horses chasing after dogs, who were chasing a fox. She hoped the fox got away. The toilet had a padded seat, which she thought the most remarkable thing of all. After using it, she washed with soap that smelled like a forest. She dried her hands with a fancy soft towel.

"I like your house," she said to her image in the mirror, trying out what she thought might please Carlotta. But she wasn't sure she did like it. She didn't have anything to compare it with, and, like all houses, it suffered from being immobile. She folded the towel and returned it to its rack. She decided she'd know what to say when she saw her aunt. She opened the door, turned off the light, and stepped out into the path of a tall, thin woman who brought herself to an abrupt halt.

"You must be Henrietta," she said in a voice with sharp, clear edges. "Well, of course you are. Who else would you be?" She was wearing a long lavender-colored dress. Her hair was red.

"You must be Carlotta," Henrietta said.

"Call me Aunt Carlotta," she said. "You brought me flowers."

"I picked them myself."

"They're lovely."

"They were growing by the side of the road."

Carlotta inspected her niece.

Henrietta didn't particularly like being examined as though she was something for sale.

"You're pretty," Carlotta said, like it came as a surprise.

"I am not," Henrietta said.

"It's a compliment to tell a girl she's pretty."

It was not that Henrietta hadn't thought about it. If she

was pretty, and she wasn't at all sure she was, that would be okay. But it wasn't something you earned, so she didn't think it was worth much.

"Hasn't anyone ever told you that before?" Carlotta asked.

"I'm a clown," Henrietta replied.

"You're a young lady."

"I'm twelve and I'm a clown."

"Just like your father." Carlotta sounded mildly exasperated.

"I'm one of the Hornbuckles," Henrietta said. "There are three of us. You can see us tonight. You can bring Fenimore." She reached into her pocket for the tickets she'd brought.

"Hello, Carlotta." Hortense was standing in the library doorway. MoMo was next to her.

Henrietta saw her aunt's expression flicker with regret before she broke into another big smile. The sisters sized each other up.

"You look good," Hortense said.

"So do you," Carlotta said.

"I am," Hortense said.

"So am I," Carlotta said. "I've changed."

"So I see," Hortense said. "You hardly seem the same at all."

"I've been looking forward to this," Carlotta said. She focused her attention on MoMo. "I'm glad to see you, if you can believe that. Which I'm sure you can't."

"I'll give it my best shot," MoMo said.

"How'd you get such a big house?" Henrietta asked. She got another poke from her mother.

"That's easy," Carlotta said. "My late husband, Barnaby Max, the car-wash king of Nassau county, left me very well-off." She propelled herself down the hall. "Follow me. Fenimore will serve tea in the gazebo."

"What's a gazebo?" Henrietta asked.

"A playhouse for grownups," Carlotta said.

75

TEATIME

They crossed the large rectangular yard with its huge copper beech tree and precisely kept flower beds, then climbed the several steps up into the six-sided, one-room house with no walls.

"I like your gazebo," Henrietta said. She thought that might please her aunt.

"I like it too," Carlotta said.

They sat at a table which was set with a white cloth, cups on saucers, plates, spoons, forks, and white cloth napkins. A silver teapot, sugar bowl, and creamer sat on an ornate silver tray.

"The garden is beautiful," Hortense said.

"It's my passion," Carlotta said.

"Who are all the people in the paintings?" Henrietta asked.

"I don't have the slightest idea," Carlotta said. "Barnaby

and I bought a hundred of them and hung them all over the house."

"I could go inside and help Fenimore," Henrietta said. It seemed to her that it was taking a long time for the food to arrive.

"Fenimore does quite well on his own," Carlotta said.

"Maybe I could help him go faster," Henrietta said.

Just then Fenimore appeared. He made his way to the gazebo carrying another silver tray. He set it down, then poured tea, then offered cream and sugar. Henrietta took both. Next came the sandwiches.

"Cucumber and butter," Fenimore said. He held the tray for Carlotta. "Also, smoked salmon and dill." She took one of each, as did Hortense and MoMo.

"They're small," Henrietta said, eyeing the tray. The sandwiches were bite-size.

"Take as many as you like," Carlotta said.

"What happened to the crusts?" Henrietta asked.

"We feed them to the birds," Carlotta said.

"I like the crusts," Henrietta said.

"So do the birds," Carlotta said.

Henrietta took three of each.

Fenimore placed the tray in the center of the table. "Will there be anything else, madam?"

"Not unless you can think of something," Carlotta said.

"Nothing at the moment, madam," Fenimore said. He made his way back across the yard.

Carlotta, Hortense, and MoMo nibbled at their sand-wiches. Henrietta popped one into her mouth, then another, then another. She thought there wasn't nearly enough between the slices, which were wafer thin.

"I was surprised to get your letter," Carlotta said.

"It was time," Hortense said. "Long overdue."

"How did you find me?" Carlotta asked.

"I called Gretchen," Hortense said. "She has the address of every member of your class."

"She never got over having to graduate," Carlotta said. "How is she?"

"The same, I think," Hortense said. "It wasn't a long conversation."

"We should take a walk," MoMo said to his daughter.

Henrietta thought that was an excellent idea.

"You'll find Fenimore in the kitchen if you're still hun-gry," Carlotta said.

Henrietta thought that was an even better idea. Her stomach was growling. She gave her mother a hug, then headed inside with her father. They found Fenimore work-ing his way through a roast beef sandwich on rye bread.

"Help yourself," Fenimore said, indicating the plate of sandwiches on the table.

Henrietta sat and started eating. MoMo took half a sand-wich and sat next to his daughter. Fenimore asked them about the circus. MoMo gave him a rundown. They asked him where he was from, which turned out to be many parts of the world. He asked them about being a clown. Henrietta told him how much she loved it, then asked why Fenimore worked for Carlotta.

"Because she needs me," Fenimore said.

"Why does she need you?" Henrietta asked.

"Because she's not much good at doing things for herself," Fenimore said. "I only work for people who need me. As opposed to those who only think they do."

"What's it like to live in such a big house?" Henrietta asked.

"I live in the apartment above the garage," Fenimore said.

"She lives here all by herself?" Henrietta asked. "In all these rooms?"

"We're leaving!" Hortense suddenly yelled from the hall.

Henrietta and MoMo shot to their feet, thanked Fenimore, and ran after her.

"I'll drive you," Fenimore said, running after them.

"What happened?" Henrietta asked when she'd caught up with her mother.

"I don't want to talk about it," Hortense said. Her voice resonated with anger.

"Then we won't," MoMo said.

Fenimore beat them to the door and opened it. "I'd really like to drive you," he said as they charged past him.

Hortense headed for the street.

Fenimore ran to the garage.

"What did she say?" Henrietta asked.

"I said I didn't want to talk about it." Hortense lengthened her stride. "It doesn't matter. I'm me and she's her and that's not going to change."

Henrietta saw a large, square, ancient-looking car pull out into the street. It was high off the ground and painted a lustrous black. What appeared to be a silver angel was attached to its prow.

"Please let me drive you," Fenimore pleaded from the open window as he pulled even with them. "It would mean a great deal."

Henrietta thought there was something strange about the car, then saw what it was. The steering wheel was on the side where the passenger was supposed to be. She wanted to ride in a car like that.

"I'd like to see the circus," Fenimore said.

"Come on," Henrietta prodded. "What do you say? We're not mad at Fenimore."

"I often take the car for a spin," Fenimore said. "Madam won't miss me."

"We won't get to ride in something like this again," MoMo said, as eager as his daughter to try it out.

"Let's do it," Henrietta said.

"Oh, all right," Hortense said, stopping in her tracks.

Fenimore braked the car and hurried to open the back door. Hortense climbed in, followed by MoMo, then Henrietta. Fenimore got in behind the wheel.

"Thank you," he said. "Henrietta, pull down the seat behind me."

Henrietta figured out the jump seat and opened it. She sat facing her parents, who were nestled into what looked like a small couch.

"Off we go then," Fenimore said.

Henrietta felt the car pull smoothly forward. "Why is the steering wheel on the wrong side?" she asked.

"The car comes from England," Fenimore replied. "It's a Rolls-Royce. Over there they drive on the other side of the road."

"They must have a lot of accidents," Henrietta said.

"No more than the usual amount," Fenimore said. "They think we drive on the wrong side over here."

Henrietta took in her surroundings. Her first house, now her first car ride. The seats were leather. The trim was dark, rich wood. Lace curtains covered the side windows. She shifted her gaze to her mother. Hortense was staring straight ahead, as though she'd absented herself.

"I'm sure that whatever madam said, she already regrets it," Fenimore said over his shoulder.

Henrietta couldn't tell if her mother was upset by this remark or interested in hearing more. She saw her father getting ready to intercede.

"Madam tries hard not to say the first thing that occurs to her," Fenimore continued. "She often forgets, which is when she gets into trouble. I've encouraged her to wait for the second thing to occur before speaking. Her better qualities emerge when she does that. Perhaps you might consider giving her another opportunity."

THE WALK HOME

The Rolls-Royce pulled into the field and parked by the caravan. Hortense went immediately to the RV. MoMo thanked Fenimore and hustled after his wife.

"Carlotta stinks," Henrietta said.

"Madam can be harsh at times," Fenimore said. "But she can make up for it."

"She made my mother feel bad," Henrietta said. "She stinks. I don't care if she says the first thing or the tenth thing. She still stinks."

Ixnay appeared, drawn like a magnet to the magnificence of the machine. He grinned like a kid as he circled it. "What's the horsepower?" he asked finally.

"A more than sufficient amount," Fenimore replied.

Ixnay nodded his appreciation. Fenimore released the

hood and raised it, exposing a gleaming engine. Ixnay stepped forward to conduct his examination.

"This automobile is a tribute to mechanical excellence we won't see again," Ixnay said to Henrietta. "We don't build things to last anymore."

The other clowns had gathered by then, and Henrietta introduced them to Fenimore. She showed him the stage and the props she and MoMo used for the mirror act. Grouchy let him try on a frizzy wig. Notz gave him a red bulb nose as a keepsake.

"I have to get ready for tonight," Henrietta said. "I want to give you these." She handed Fenimore the two tickets she'd intended for Carlotta. "Maybe you know somebody you can bring."

Fenimore thanked her, put the red bulb nose in his pocket, and drove off. Henrietta met her mother coming out of the RV. She was made up and in costume.

"I'll get over it," Hortense said. She smiled, but Henrietta could tell she'd been crying.

MoMo was painting on his face.

"There you are, dear girl," he said. "Your mother is feeling better."

"She doesn't look better."

"She's disappointed."

Henrietta stripped to her underwear, then stepped into her baggy pants and suspenders. She sat next to her father and began painting her face. "What did Carlotta say to her?"

"Your mother wouldn't tell me, but I'd bet anything it had to do with me, and possibly you turning out like me."

"What's wrong with that?" Henrietta couldn't think of anything more splendid.

"Not a thing," MoMo said. "If Carlotta said anything about you, she got an earful, I can guarantee that."

Henrietta felt bad about what had happened, but there was nothing to be done. Her mother had tried and been rejected. Maybe now she'd remember why she left that world. Maybe she'd let the future take care of itself.

"She thought enough time had passed," MoMo said. "She thought her sister might feel the same way. When we first got there, I thought so too. I think your mother had the idea that we could all live here and be a family."

"We already are a family," Henrietta said.

"When we settle down."

"I don't want to settle down."

"I know that, dear girl."

"I don't want to live here."

"I know that too," MoMo said. "I wake up every morning thinking this will be the day things turn around."

"We're going to stay clowns," Henrietta said.

"Always," MoMo said.

That evening, one hundred and thirty-nine paying customers witnessed a near-flawless performance of Filbert's Traveling Clown Circus. It was as though the clowns were stepping things up a level in preparation for Union Square. Even Sweetpea surprised herself by how much she put into it. They received a long and hearty ovation.

Otto, of the resale clothing outlet, brought his family backstage afterward. The clowns signed Otto Junior's program. The crowd disappeared into the night, and the clowns started breaking down the equipment. That was when Henrietta saw Carlotta. She was standing next to her car. Then Hortense saw her. Henrietta and her father watched as the sisters met and talked.

"I thought we were never going to see her again," Henrietta said. Carlotta's appearance made her uneasy. She wished she hadn't given the tickets to Fenimore.

"Life is filled with surprises," MoMo said.

"What does she want?"

"We're about to find out."

"My sister doesn't want to leave things the way they are," Hortense said when she returned. "She's invited us for ice cream, and I said yes."

"We have to help pack the equipment," Henrietta said. "It's late. We can't."

"Nobody will mind," Hortense said. "We're going."

"Ice cream it is," MoMo said.

A half hour later, changed and cleaned up, Henrietta

and MoMo sat with Fenimore in the kitchen eating blue-berry ice cream. Hortense and Carlotta were off somewhere deciding what to do about themselves.

"This is the best ice cream I ever ate," Henrietta said. Her tongue was blue. Everybody's was.

"Isn't it though," Fenimore said, smacking his lips. "A lot of blueberries and a lot of cream, that's the secret."

"You made this?" MoMo asked.

"After you left," Fenimore said.

"How did you get her to the show?" MoMo asked.

"I told her she'd never see her sister again if she didn't go," Fenimore said. "Or you, or Henrietta."

"She doesn't like us," Henrietta said.

"It's me she doesn't like," MoMo said.

"It's Madam herself who is the problem," Fenimore said. "I think she's quite taken with you." This last was directed at Henrietta.

"Why me?" Henrietta made it sound like she'd won a prize she didn't want.

"You're impossible to resist, dear girl," MoMo said.

"If she doesn't like you, she can't like me," Henrietta said. "She can't have one of us without the other."

The sisters appeared in the doorway. They seemed relaxed in each other's company. "Fenimore will drive you back," Carlotta said.

"We'll walk," MoMo said.

"It will be good for us after the ice cream," Hortense said.

"He'll collect you in the morning then," Carlotta said.

"We're coming for breakfast," Hortense said.

☙ ☙ ☙

They made their way to the road where Henrietta had picked the prickly flowers and headed home. They walked side by side by side in silence for a while, Hortense on the narrow shoulder, Henrietta in the middle, MoMo on the outside. A car cast them in its headlamps as it passed going in the opposite direction. Otherwise there was no traffic. Here and there they could see the lights of a house. They heard a dog barking, then another, then another. Henrietta wondered if it wasn't a secret code. Night creatures chirped. A sliver of pale moon played tag with slow-moving clouds.

"Carlotta's hard to get rid of," Henrietta said.

Her parents laughed.

"Well, she is."

"We're making progress," Hortense said. "She's having a hard time letting go of the past, but she's trying. She's lonely."

"Do we have to have breakfast with her?" Henrietta asked.

"We haven't finished talking," Hortense said.

"Fenimore will make it worth our while," MoMo said. "We won't eat like that once we leave."

"But we're leaving in the morning," Henrietta said. "Right after breakfast."

"We'll eat and be on our way," MoMo said.

"Good," Henrietta said, as emphatically as she could. She didn't think Carlotta was a bad person, especially if her mother didn't think so, but she was greatly relieved to know they'd be moving on when they were supposed to.

"We're going to be a big hit in Union Square," Henrietta said.

"We're going to do boffo," MoMo said. He turned suddenly, like he'd heard something behind him. Then he shoved Henrietta into Hortense, and the two of them went hard to the ground.

As Henrietta fell, time slowed, until it seemed nearly to stop altogether. Moving images became a series of still pictures. She saw her mother on her knees looking wildly about, stunned. She saw her father lying limp and still in the road. She saw the back of a car speeding away. Its lights were out.

THEN IT ALL CHANGED

Henrietta watched her mother lift her father's head and cradle it. What was happening? Why wasn't her father waking up? She realized she was shaking. She wasn't even sure she was breathing.

"Get help!" Hortense cried. "Hurry!"

Henrietta took off like a blur for the nearest house. She ran faster than she'd ever run before, too fast to think about anything. Along the road, then up a long, long driveway to the house, which was on a hill. When she got there she pounded on the door and yelled for help. When a man in a bathrobe appeared, she kept yelling. About her father. About the car with no lights. That her father needed help. In truth she wasn't sure what she said. The man in the bathrobe ran to call 911.

Henrietta ran back to the road as fast as she'd come. Her mother was still cradling her father.

"They're coming," Henrietta said. Her mouth was dry. Her throat felt closed. She sat on the ground by her parents and pressed herself against them. She could hear her father's labored breathing. It was shallow and irregular.

"He's going to be all right," Hortense said.

"He's going to be all right," Henrietta repeated.

"He has to be," Hortense said.

Henrietta leaned in closer, until her lips were touching her father's ear. "I've been thinking about the Eight-Foot-Tall," she said. "What if we faced in opposite directions? Then the audience wouldn't know if we were coming or going."

MoMo made a sound. Henrietta was certain of it.

"He laughed," she said. "He's going to be all right." She looked at her mother. "I told him a joke and he laughed." Hortense didn't seem to hear.

"How far do you think Peppy and Wanda and Boris have gotten?" Henrietta asked her father. She figured if she kept talking until help arrived, he'd stay alive. "They could be half-way. If their RV didn't break down. They don't have Ixnay to fix it. Maybe we can perform in Denver sometime and see them."

Henrietta talked about whatever she could think of. She felt the rhythm of her mother's breathing. She looked up and saw tears falling from her mother's eyes. She heard sirens. She saw flashing lights.

Paramedics gently pried the two of them away from

MoMo so they could tend to him. Flares were ignited and set out on the road. A blanket was wrapped around Henrietta, another around Hortense. A camera flashed. A policeman was taking photographs of MoMo and the surrounding area. He took one of Henrietta and Hortense. A paramedic examined them. Another policeman asked them questions. Hortense said she hadn't seen or heard the car until it was driving away. Henrietta listened as if in a fog. She tried to convince herself that it hadn't happened.

"I want my husband!" Hortense yelled. MoMo was being put into the back of the ambulance. She struggled to get in after him. "I want to go with him."

A policeman restrained her. "I'll take you to the hospital," he said.

Henrietta saw the doors to the ambulance being shut. It pulled away, quickly gaining speed. She ran after it. It disappeared from her view. She kept running. She thought her lungs would burst. A police car pulled past, then stopped. Her mother got out.

"They're taking us to the hospital to be with your father," she said.

Henrietta climbed into the backseat. The police car took off, lights flashing, siren blaring. She was barely aware of anything except that they weren't going fast enough. She needed to be there. Her father would be all right if she was with him.

MoMo was being worked on when they arrived at the

emergency room. A young doctor examined them and found only scrapes and bruises, which were cleaned and dressed. The doctor gave Hortense a small envelope of pills.

"These will help you sleep," he said. "You can give your daughter a half if she needs it."

"I don't need anything," Henrietta said.

The doctor explained about shock and how it didn't set in sometimes for hours, or even days. If they had any problems they were to come back immediately.

Henrietta sat quietly next to her mother while they waited for MoMo's doctor. Nobody would tell them anything except that Mr. Hornbuckle was receiving the best care possible. A policeman asked more questions. Henrietta tried to remember what the back of the car looked like.

"It was dark," she said. "The car didn't have any lights on. There wasn't any noise." She wondered why the driver hadn't seen them. Why hadn't they heard the car coming? Then it struck her that her father had saved their lives by pushing them off the road. He'd heard something, but it had been too late.

A gray-haired woman in green surgical scrubs came through a set of swinging doors. Hortense shot to her feet. Henrietta jumped to her mother's side.

The doctor took Hortense's hand. "I'm sorry," she said. "We did everything we could. He was too far gone when he came in." She looked down at Henrietta.

"I'm sorry," she said again.

"Sorry?" Henrietta blurted. She saw the horror on her mother's face. She felt herself being pulled to her mother's side.

"He never regained consciousness," the doctor said. "There wasn't any pain."

They were talking about her father like he was dead. That wasn't possible. She'd heard him laugh. She'd heard him breathing. She felt her mother's hand slip away.

Hortense sagged. The doctor caught her. The policeman helped. "I'm all right," she said.

"Sit down for a few minutes," the doctor said.

"No," Hortense said. "I want to see my husband." She broke free from the doctor's hold and squared her shoulders. "Take me to him, please."

"I'm coming too," Henrietta said.

Hortense held out her hand. "We'll see him together."

The doctor led them to a corner of the emergency room where a curtain had been drawn around a bed. It isn't real so it doesn't matter, Henrietta thought. I'll wake up and it will be over. She felt her mother holding on tighter.

"His major injuries were internal," the doctor said. "We did everything we could." She pulled back the curtain.

MoMo was covered to his chin with a blanket. His eyes were closed. There was a bruise on his chin and a cut on his forehead. Otherwise he looked like he'd always looked.

"I'll give you a few minutes," the doctor said. She left, pulling the curtain closed around them.

Henrietta wanted MoMo to open his eyes and get up so they could go home. She watched her mother whisper something into her father's ear, then kiss him on the lips. When it was her turn, she stood on her toes so she could get close enough to whisper something of her own.

"When I wake up," she told her father, "you'll be there." She kissed him, then inhaled as deeply as she could to capture the smell of him, because she knew it would have to last.

❂ ❂ ❂

The clowns gathered around the police car when it pulled in by the caravan. They stood silently as Henrietta and Hortense got out.

"Where's MoMo?" Wilhelmenia asked.

"He didn't get himself arrested, did he?" Ixnay asked.

"He was hit by a car," Hortense said in a quiet, still voice. She waited for what seemed forever before telling them the rest of it.

Henrietta thought she was going to be sick. Then she thought she was going crazy. One by one the clowns came forward and embraced her and then her mother. All of them were crying. She couldn't bear it. This happened to other people. It happened in books. She went to the RV and sat on the couch and stared out the open door. She couldn't believe her father was never going to walk through it again, calling out her name, telling her they had to get ready for the show. Instead, her mother came in and closed the door.

"I haven't asked about you," she said. "I don't know what to ask. Or what to say."

"I'm fine," Henrietta said.

"No you're not," Hortense said. "I'm not either. I'm angry and scared and my heart is broken. I'm so tired I think I'll fall over."

"I'm fine," Henrietta insisted again.

"Are you hungry? I'll fix you something."

"I'm not hungry."

"Do you want to talk about it?"

"No."

"We'll both have to talk sometime," Hortense said.

"I want to go to bed," Henrietta said.

"Me too," Hortense said. "I'm going to take one of those pills the doctor gave us. Do you want half?"

"I don't need anything."

"You can sleep with me if you don't want to be alone."

"This is my bed," Henrietta said.

"I'll be better in the morning," Hortense said. "If you need me, wake me up." She kissed her daughter, then hugged her.

Henrietta let herself be taken into her mother's arms, but she gave nothing back. She felt cold.

"Promise me you'll wake me if you need anything," her mother said.

Henrietta didn't respond.

"Promise me. I can't go to sleep unless you do."

"I promise," Henrietta said.

Hortense went to the tiny chamber she'd shared with her husband. She left the door open.

Henrietta went through her nightly ritual by the num-bers. She peed and washed and brushed her teeth. She took her hair out of its ponytail and brushed it. She stripped to her underwear, then converted the couch into a bed. She lay down and closed her eyes, never expecting to fall asleep again. Then she was deep in a dream. She was walking on a deserted road. It was night. She was being followed. She kept looking back. Nothing was there. She started running. The road got longer.

THE FIRST DAY OF EVERYTHING ELSE

hen she woke, Henrietta saw her mother sitting in a chair watching her.

"Good morning, Henrietta Hornbuckle," Hortense said. She tried a smile that didn't quite make it. She was dressed and wearing lipstick. Her makeup couldn't hide the fact that she'd been crying.

"We have to be strong," Hortense said. "We have to help each other. There are arrangements to be made for your father, then we have to decide about ourselves. Get dressed. We'll have breakfast."

"I'm not hungry," Henrietta said.

"Neither am I," her mother said, "but we have to eat. We have to let our friends be sad with us. They lost somebody they loved too. Don't be long."

Henrietta could hear the clowns gathering outside. She could smell bacon cooking on the grill. She didn't want to eat and she didn't want to see anyone. She didn't want to do anything. Why should she? Nothing mattered anymore. But MoMo would want her to get out of bed. "There is work to be done and there are hearts to be won," her father would have said. She washed and dressed and stepped outside to face a bright, sunny, warm, uncertain, terrifying new day.

98

Her mother was sitting with the others around the table, sipping her coffee, listening as they spoke.

Ixnay came to have a private word. "Your father was the greatest man I ever knew," he said.

Each of them had a word with Henrietta. She didn't know how to respond, so she said nothing. The whispered words of grief and encouragement fell on her like gentle rain. When they were done, she sat with her mother. Guillermo set a plate of pancakes and bacon on the table. Henrietta wolfed them down. She didn't object when a second helping was offered.

"This is the saddest day in the history of Filbert's Traveling Clown Circus since my own dear Filbert passed over," Wilhelmenia said when breakfast was done. "MoMo was the biggest man I ever knew. He was our heart. Our sympathy goes out to Hortense and Henrietta for their loss, which we deeply share."

Henrietta saw Wilhelmenia looking at her and her mother. They were all looking.

"We'd like to have a memorial service, if that's all right," Wilhelmenia said. "We'd like to honor him."

Hortense nodded her approval.

"We'd like to have a party afterward," Wilhelmenia continued, "to celebrate his life."

"That's exactly what we should do," Grandmother Spangle said.

The others agreed.

Again, Hortense nodded.

Henrietta saw how hard her mother was working to keep from falling apart.

"There's one more thing," Wilhelmenia said. "The circus has to close."

Henrietta shook her head back and forth like a pain was shooting through her brain. What did Wilhelmenia mean, close the circus? For a few days? Longer? Maybe she hadn't heard right.

"The reserve fund is long gone," Wilhelmenia continued. "Even if we started doing a lot better right away, it wouldn't be enough. We need new everything. We can't afford anything. Without MoMo there isn't any reason to try. We've done our last show."

How could they let what her father had loved so much just stop being? Henrietta waited for somebody to say something, to register the first objection, but nobody did. She wanted to scream that they were all wrong, that MoMo would want them to keep the circus going no matter what, but she didn't have the strength. She felt powerless, like her body was being crushed.

The Rolls-Royce pulled in. Ixnay took Fenimore aside and told him what had happened. Fenimore spoke briefly with Hortense, then with Henrietta, expressing his disbelief, telling each how sorry he was. He drove off to tell Carlotta.

Grandmother Spangle started talking about some of the extraordinary things she'd seen MoMo do. "He was a great actor," she said. "He could sell an audience anything."

"He had a fine singing voice," Lola said.

"He was as good a dancer as I've ever seen," Guillermo said.

"There was nothing he couldn't do on the stage," Ixnay said.

"There was only one MoMo," Wilhelmenia said.

The clowns started telling stories about MoMo's talent and his generous nature. Soon they were smiling. Then Guillermo laughed. Henrietta saw that her mother liked hearing the stories. They seemed to comfort her. She slipped away and returned to the RV. She sat at the makeup table and stared into the mirror, thinking if she stared long enough her father would appear in it at her side. They could paint their faces together and talk a little.

When that didn't happen, she closed her eyes and tried to imagine them doing the mirror act. She saw them on opposite sides of the empty picture frame, shaving their faces with enormous rubber razors. Then the image disappeared. She opened her eyes and looked around, then squeezed them shut as hard as she could to bring the image back. All she saw were pinwheels of color.

She heard Fenimore outside. A few moments later her mother and Carlotta came in.

"I'm so sorry," Carlotta said. "I don't know what to say. It's so sad."

Henrietta looked away. She didn't want her aunt here. She wanted her to leave. She kept her lips pressed together so she wouldn't upset her mother.

"I'll make tea," Hortense said.

"Don't be silly," Carlotta said.

"It will give me something to do." Hortense put the kettle on.

"Have you decided on the arrangements?" Carlotta sat on the couch.

Henrietta watched her aunt looking around the RV with a frown of disapproval.

"We talked about it once," Hortense said. "We agreed that we both wanted to be cremated when the time came." She blew her nose.

Carlotta tilted her head toward Henrietta. "Isn't she young for this conversation?"

"I know what being cremated is," Henrietta said. "Guillermo showed me pictures of how they do it in India. The Vikings used to do their funerals that way. Just because I'm twelve doesn't mean I don't know what's going on."

"You'll forgive my ignorance," Carlotta said.

"My father wouldn't want to be buried in a hole in the ground either," Henrietta said. "He'd want to keep moving."

"We're out of milk," Hortense said, handing her sister a mug of tea. "We have sugar."

"This will do," Carlotta said. She played with the tea bag's string. "Whatever you want, tell them at the funeral home." She handed Hortense a business card. "They're the people who buried Barnaby."

"Thank you," Hortense said, trying to hand the card back. "We can't afford it."

"They'll send me the bill," Carlotta said. "There's nothing to discuss in that regard. You'll let me do this for you. Please. There's a lot I'd like to do. A lot to make up for." She put the mug down, the tea untouched, and stood.

"Fenimore will drive you wherever you want to go," she said. "He'll bring you for dinner tonight." She gave them both a long sympathetic look, then left.

"Why are you letting her help us?" Henrietta demanded of her mother. "She didn't like my father. She doesn't like me."

"That's not true," Hortense said. "And the past is gone. And there's nothing I can do about it. You can be as mad as you want. I'm so angry I think I'll go out of my mind. But not at my sister. She hasn't done anything wrong."

Her mother grabbed Henrietta suddenly and held on tightly. Henrietta put her arms around her mother's neck, but she still couldn't let herself give in to her feelings. Because none of it seemed real. Because she was too numb to feel anything. Because she was determined not to have any feelings at all.

"We'll get through this," her mother said.

"I want my father to come with us," Henrietta said. "I want him to stay with the circus."

"There is no circus," her mother said.

"There is," Henrietta insisted.

"You have to accept that it's over," Hortense said.

"I want him to come with us," Henrietta repeated.

Her mother took hold of her by the shoulders. "You can't keep doing this, Henrietta. It's hard enough. We have to deal with what we have."

There was a knock at the door. A detective identified himself. "I have your husband's personal effects," he said. He handed Hortense a brown envelope. He told them they were examining MoMo and his clothing for evidence that might lead them to the car. He said they didn't hold out much hope. MoMo's body would be released tomorrow. Hortense told the detective the name of the funeral home. He said they'd do everything they could to find the creep who did it.

"Everyone on the force is sorry about this," he said.

Henrietta watched her mother open the envelope. She removed MoMo's wallet, the few dollars he'd been carrying, his wedding ring, and his wristwatch, an old Timex with a sweep second hand and a black leather band.

"It's still running," her mother said. "Would you like it?"

Henrietta felt herself choking up. She hadn't cried. She didn't want to. She didn't know why. She fastened the watch to the inside of her left wrist, so that she had to turn her hand palm up to read the time, just as her father had. She put it to her ear. She could hear the faint ticking of time moving forward.

104

"It fits," was all she could say.

Hortense nodded, unable to speak.

Lola and Guillermo appeared at the door, wanting to know if it was a good time to visit. Hortense was happy for the company.

Henrietta went looking for Wilhelmenia. She was in the back of her RV, sorting through sheet music.

"I'm putting something together for your father's memorial," Wilhelmenia said. She swiveled in her chair and fixed Henrietta with a smile.

"When I lost Filbert I thought my life was over," she said. "But I learned it wasn't. Just a lot sadder. It takes time, but life goes on. MoMo would expect you to do that. He thought you were capable of anything."

"Then we can keep the circus open," Henrietta said.

"Is that so?" Wilhelmenia raised an eyebrow.

"It is if we want it to be."

"And how would we do that?"

"We'll just keep going until things get better, then there won't be any more problems."

"If you spend more than you make, what happens?" Wilhelmenia asked.

"You make adjustments."

"And after you've made the adjustments and you're still spending more than you're making, what then?"

"Make more adjustments," Henrietta said.

"Until you adjust yourself right out of business," Wilhelmenia said. "You know as well as I do what I'm saying."

"If my father was alive we wouldn't close."

"We were going to try to make it south and quit there," Wilhelmenia said. "MoMo and I agreed on that being the end."

"He never said anything to me."

"He didn't want to tell you until the last possible moment. He knew how hard you'd take it."

"We can keep it going until then and see what happens."

"We can't," Wilhelmenia said. "We don't have money for food. I've been paying for it since we got to Long Island."

"We didn't vote on it," Henrietta said. "We're supposed to vote on everything."

"Nobody objected."

"That's not the same," Henrietta said, knowing Wilhelmenia didn't have to give in if she didn't want to.

"All right," Wilhelmenia said. "Technically we didn't vote. I'll let you pass the word."

Henrietta found Grandmother Spangle carefully packing away her lights. She made her sales pitch about how

MoMo would have wanted the circus to keep going, and that there was going to be a vote. Grandmother Spangle said she'd give the matter serious consideration.

Grouchy and Notz were on their way into town. They invited Henrietta to come with them. "We're going to get ourselves the biggest ice cream sundaes we can find," Notz said.

"Really big ones," Grouchy said. "Our treat."

As tempted as she was, Henrietta declined. She told them about the vote, and they agreed to think about it.

Ixnay told her that MoMo's watch looked good on her wrist, and that he was glad to see it there. He said he'd give the future of Filbert's his undivided attention.

So did Lola and Guillermo, who said their years with the circus had been the happiest of their lives.

She went to find Sweetpea. Sweetpea found her first. "I've been looking everywhere for you," Sweetpea said.

"We're going to have a vote on keeping the circus open," Henrietta said, wondering what she wanted.

"I know where there's a secret beach," Sweetpea said. "Come on."

"What's that got to do with the circus?" Henrietta asked as she followed along behind Sweetpea. "I know you don't want to be a clown anymore, but you could vote yes anyway."

"Which means I'd still be a clown," Sweetpea said. "Which, as you just pointed out, is something I no longer care to be. Why do you want it so much? You could be a million other things."

"Then I wouldn't be a clown," Henrietta said.

"There's a lot to choose from," Sweetpea said, "but you have to be out in the world to know what's what."

"I'm a clown inside," Henrietta said.

Sweetpea shook her head like Henrietta had lost her ability to reason.

Henrietta decided not to pursue it. Clearly Sweetpea wasn't going to change her mind. The vote would be close, but she was certain she'd win. They walked in silence until they reached the scallop-shaped bit of rock and sand that faced the bay.

"What if you already have what you want?" Henrietta asked after they'd been sitting there awhile.

"How can you know that?" Sweetpea replied. "All you've ever been is a clown."

"I just know," Henrietta said.

Sweetpea dug her heels into the sand. "I have a photograph of my father holding me when I was a baby. It's the only one of us together. He's smiling, like I made him happy."

"Of course you made him happy," Henrietta said.

"You made MoMo happy," she said. "I watched him watching you perform. I saw it in his face how much he loved you."

Henrietta picked up a stone and lobbed it into the water. It made a small splash. She watched a sailboat coming about.

"I miss MoMo too," Sweetpea said. She kissed Henrietta on the cheek, then stood and headed back.

Henrietta stayed to skip stones and think. What Sweet-pea said had made her feel a little better, but it had made her feel sad as well, and she didn't like that. And there was something eating at her. She tried to talk herself out of it, then headed for the road where her father had been hit by the car. She needed to make sense of what had happened.

She looked for the house she'd run to for help, but in the light of day she couldn't be sure which one it was. The residue from the police flares had blown away in the wind. There were no signs that anything had happened here at all. She chose a place to sit back off the road in the rough grass. She closed her eyes and focused, trying to see what had happened last night. She saw the three of them walking. She saw her father starting to look behind him. She felt him knocking her and her mother to the ground. She saw her father lying in the road. She saw the car with no lights speeding away. She opened her eyes as a car sped past in front of her.

❧ ❧ ❧

That evening when Fenimore came to pick them up for dinner at Carlotta's, Henrietta refused to go. Her mother asked twice. Henrietta wouldn't budge. She wasn't going. Hortense started to get angry, then relented.

"You don't have to if you feel so strongly about it," she said. "Not tonight anyway. I'll see you in a little while. You'll be all right?"

"Yes," Henrietta said.

"If you need anything . . ."

"I don't," she said.

"I have to hear you say it."

"If I need anything I'll go to Wilhelmenia," Henrietta said. She watched Fenimore help her mother into the car. There are only two Hornbuckles now, she thought.

A TRIBUTE TO MOMO

For the first few moments after Henrietta woke up she thought it was just another day. Then she remembered. After breakfast, her mother went off to discuss MoMo's memorial and party with Wilhelmenia. Both events were being held at Carlotta's. Henrietta had objected. She'd wanted it all to happen at the caravan, with only clowns in attendance.

"My sister offered and I said yes," her mother had responded to her complaints. "There's nothing to discuss."

Henrietta sat at the makeup table and studied herself in the mirror, willing her father's image to appear next to hers. After a while, when it didn't happen, she painted on the white clown face they'd worn doing their act together. She didn't know why she did this. She couldn't stop herself.

"Wash that off," her mother ordered when she saw what her daughter had done.

"I'm a clown," Henrietta said.

"You're a clown when you perform. You're not per-forming."

"It makes me feel better," Henrietta said. She realized that wearing a face her father had worn made her feel safer.

Hortense sat and recaptured her composure. "You look just like him," she said finally. "I could barely tell you apart in costume."

"That's why," Henrietta said, "because it makes me feel like him."

"It's hard to know what to do," Hortense said. "Maybe there's no such thing as the right way. Maybe there's just the only way you can do it."

"I'm okay," Henrietta said, thinking it might make her mother feel better to hear her say so.

"No you're not," her mother said. "Neither am I. You'll wash it off later."

"Later," Henrietta said. She felt like she'd slipped into her father's skin.

She spent the morning electioneering to keep the circus going.

❖ ❖ ❖

At eleven, Fenimore came to drive them to the Blatz Bro-thers' Funeral Home. He made no mention of Henrietta's clown face.

"I've brought something," he said, removing a lacquered box with a silver lock from the backseat of the Rolls-Royce.

He opened its lid. The inside was lined with silver and held two keys on silver chains.

"I acquired it when I was a merchant seaman," he said. "I thought it would do for MoMo's ashes."

"It's beautiful," Hortense said.

112

It was exactly what Henrietta had in mind. She knew exactly where it would go in the RV.

Fenimore returned the box to the backseat. Hortense and Henrietta climbed in. As they drove off, Henrietta put her hand on the box. She thought about what it was going to hold. She felt a shiver run through her body. She felt her mother's hand on top of hers.

They were met by the youngest Blatz brother, Dexter, on the front porch of the three-story white house. He had a crew cut and wore a gray suit and red socks.

"I'm sorry for your loss," Dexter Blatz said. "It's a terrible tragedy." He looked at Henrietta without giving the slightest indication that he found anything unusual about her clown face.

"I've heard wonderful things about your father," he said. He led them to the parlor. He offered coffee, tea, or bottled water. They declined.

Henrietta wondered why anybody would want to make a living taking care of dead people. Then she thought it probably wasn't any stranger than what clowns did to make people laugh. There weren't that many clowns, after all. Not with their own circus.

"My father should be in one of his costumes," Henrietta said.

"No costume," Hortense said. "He'll wear his best clothes."

Dexter Blatz cleared his throat.

"My husband will be dressed properly when he's cremated," Hortense said. "This will be done with dignity."

"In every respect," Dexter Blatz said. "I assure you." He made a note, then assured Hortense once more that it would be exactly as she wished.

"He should be wearing his makeup, then," Henrietta said.

"Your father was more than a clown," Hortense said. "So are you. I wish you'd get that through your head. No makeup."

"I gather you've brought the box for Mr. Hornbuckle's ashes," Dexter Blatz said.

Henrietta was hit with a horrible feeling in her stomach about her father being burned up. She reminded herself of what she'd been told, that MoMo's body wasn't MoMo anymore. She started thinking of it like a Viking funeral, where the body is put on a boat that's set on fire and pushed out to sea.

"It's what we'd like to use," Hortense said.

Dexter Blatz inspected the box, then deemed it more than suitable. "It's lovely," he said.

❂ ❂ ❂

The vote was held after lunch. Henrietta stood on a chair and asked the clowns to keep the circus going until they absolutely, positively couldn't anymore.

As much as it pained her, Wilhelmenia informed the clowns that they were past the point Henrietta had described. There was no money. There was nothing to keep going with. The vote was ten to one to close. Not one other clown, not even her mother, had sided with her. Henrietta walked away bewildered and angry, as though she'd been cut loose from her last mooring. Hortense came after her.

"Why didn't you vote yes?" Henrietta asked.

"Because I want us to close," her mother said. "The sooner we get on with our lives, the easier it will be."

"If the circus closes, how will people know who my father was?"

"You'll know," she said. "I'll know. When you have children you'll tell them."

"I'm the one who talked him into going to Carlotta's," Henrietta said. "I told him I wanted to meet her. Now I wish I hadn't."

Her mother hushed her. She knelt and looked right into her eyes. "There's no guilt or blame for anybody but the driver of that car," she said. "We can't change what happened. You have to wash off that makeup." She wrapped her arms around her daughter.

❂   ❂   ❂

The next morning Henrietta strapped on her father's watch and painted her clown face back on. She'd told her mother she wouldn't, but she had to. When Hortense saw what she'd done, she yelled at her to wash it off at once.

"Just for today," Henrietta pleaded. "After that I won't need it anymore."

"No more after today," her mother said, relenting.

"I'll take it off after the memorial," Henrietta said.

Hortense went to her bedroom and returned holding the burgundy shirt with the pearly buttons and the yellow butterfly stitched on the back. "Your father was going to surprise you."

Henrietta removed the shirt she was wearing, put on her father's gift, and buttoned the pearly buttons. She thought it went well with her red and white striped shorts.

"Your father was right," Hortense said. "It has your name written all over it."

They heard the Rolls-Royce pull up outside the RV. Fenimore was there to take them to the funeral home.

Dexter Blatz met them on the porch. He led them to the lacquered box that now held MoMo's remains. He handed Hortense and Henrietta each a key. Henrietta put the chain around her neck. While her mother and Dexter Blatz talked, she laid her hands on the box. Her father was inside. One part of him. The physical proof that Morris Mortimer Hornbuckle had once existed.

❖   ❖   ❖

By the time they arrived at Carlotta's, the clowns had gathered in the yard. Henrietta carried MoMo's box to the gazebo. She set it on the table, where it could be seen. Wilhelmenia began playing a medley of circus songs on her electric calliope, which was connected to an extension cord that ran through an open window into the house.

"I'll serve the refreshments when you're ready," Fenimore said to Hortense. She invited him to stay for the memorial.

"I'd like that," he said.

"Ask my sister to join us," Hortense said.

Fenimore went to get her. Henrietta wasn't happy, but she thought it was probably a good idea because Carlotta was being nice to her mother. Her father would have liked that. Wilhelmenia played music that Henrietta had heard her entire life, but it sounded different. It was slower, sadder. Fenimore returned with Carlotta.

Each clown rose and went to the gazebo. Each shared a brief personal story. Each touched MoMo's box, then sat again. Henrietta and Hortense were last.

Hortense spoke about her husband, about how much he loved being a clown, about how much he loved the circus and all of them, and most of all how much he'd loved his daughter.

Then it was Henrietta's turn. She put her hand on MoMo's box. She wanted to say something special that would change everything back to the way it had been a few days ago. She wanted to do it all over again so it would turn out differently. But she knew there were no magic words. There was only uncertainty. And her idea.

"The way to honor my father," Henrietta said, "is for us to perform at Union Square."

She saw the clowns looking at her like they weren't sure they'd heard correctly. Wilhelmenia started shaking her head. She was clearly distressed. Her mother was looking at her with surprise.

"MoMo never got to perform in New York City," Henrietta said. "It meant more to him than anything. We should go to Union Square. We should do one more show. That should be my father's memorial."

The clowns looked at one another and murmured among themselves. Henrietta couldn't tell what was happening. Then she saw the smiles.

"We can certainly do one more performance," Ixnay said. "I'm for it."

"It's something we'd never forget," Guillermo said.

"We can wait to disband until after that," Notz said.

"It's a brilliant idea," Grandmother Spangle said.

"One more show," Henrietta said to her mother.

"One more show," Hortense said, barely able to hold back her tears.

Henrietta could see Carlotta chewing on it, like she was waiting for the second thing to say. Or maybe even the third.

"All in favor?" Lola yelled.

"We can't," Wilhelmenia bellowed above the excitement. "I canceled our appearance. It's too late."

"It's never too late," Grouchy said.

"Call them," Ixnay said.

"Maybe they didn't give our spot away," Grandmother Spangle said.

"Get it back if they did," Sweetpea said.

"Do whatever you have to," Grouchy said.

"I'll show you to the phone," Fenimore said.

Wilhelmenia rushed inside after him.

WAKING UP

enrietta felt herself being shaken. From far away she heard her mother's voice. It got closer.

"You were yelling in your sleep," Hortense said. "Are you all right?"

Henrietta nodded that she was.

"I had a dream about your father," Hortense said.

"I dreamed about him too," Henrietta replied. "We were doing the Eight-Foot-Tall in Union Square. We were a big hit. The circus got booked everywhere and we went on performing for ever and ever." She didn't tell her mother about the dream changing, about her suddenly being alone on the dark road being followed by something she couldn't see.

"I don't remember anything about my dream," Hortense said, "except that I saw him in it and he was smiling." She kissed her daughter on the head. "We're rehearsing this morning."

Henrietta saw sunlight streaming in through the windows. She looked over at MoMo's box sitting on the makeup table. "There is work to be done and there are hearts to be won," she said aloud.

The show had to be reorganized. MoMo had been such an integral part of so much of it, nearly all of it had to be altered in some way. At the morning meeting it was decided that Henrietta would take her father's place in those acts where MoMo had been one of the group rather than the featured attraction. That gave Henrietta a lot to do. It gave her less time to ponder.

Guillermo said he'd take MoMo's place in the Cinderella act. Lola said she'd play Cinderella. Grouchy became the prince's trusted vassal.

"My mother and I will do the mirror act," Henrietta said.

"I can't," Hortense protested. "I don't know it well enough."

"Yes you do," Henrietta said. "You've seen it a thousand times."

"I'm too tall," her mother said. "It won't look right."

"I'll stand and you'll sit," Henrietta said. "I'll help you with the makeup."

"I can light it so you look the same," Grandmother Spangle said.

"Who'll do the music?" Hortense asked.

Sweetpea raised her hand.

Henrietta shot her a smile of thanks.

Sweetpea shrugged it off like it was no big thing.

"I want us to have something we did together," Henrietta said to her mother, laying on her most soulful look, the one designed to melt rock.

Hortense laughed.

Henrietta was so happy to hear the sound of it that she laughed herself.

"I'll give it a try," Hortense said.

"That takes care of everything but the finale," Wilhelmenia said. "Henrietta, will you lead off with the singing?"

"Yes," she said. "But there's something else. I'm going to do the Eight-Foot-Tall." The announcement got everybody's undivided attention. "Ixnay will help me figure out how."

"Maybe I can do that," Ixnay said. "Who knows what's possible?"

"I'll leave it to you," Wilhelmenia said. "If it's ready, it'll go in just before 'Pie Time!' In MoMo's bouncing-ball spot." She set the schedule of rehearsals. There would be two a day until they departed for the city.

"This will be the final performance of Filbert's Traveling Clown Circus," she said. "Let's make it the best show we've ever done."

The first chance she got after that, Henrietta sat down with Ixnay to talk about doing the Eight-Foot-Tall alone.

"You want me to turn you into an eight-foot-tall clown who comes apart in the middle," was how Ixnay summarized the challenge.

"That's it," Henrietta said. "As long as I look like one clown doing it."

Ixnay thought for a minute, then said he'd see what he could conjure up. "No promises," he said.

122

After lunch Henrietta and her mother rehearsed the mirror act. "You'll make the first moves," Henrietta said. "I'll do the reacting. Don't think about me. Don't pay attention to what I'm doing. What you do, I'll do. If you miss something, it doesn't matter. I'll cover your mistakes, if you make any, which you won't." She realized she'd just recited the speech her father had given her the first time they did it together. Word for word. Her mother knew the act better than she thought she did.

"You're going to have to put on another shirt sometime," Hortense said when they returned to the RV. Henrietta was wearing the butterfly shirt for the third straight day.

"I will," she said.

"When?"

"Soon."

"How soon?"

"Tomorrow."

"Okay," Hortense said. "Tomorrow."

"I don't want to stay with Carlotta," Henrietta said.

"I haven't decided anything yet."

"I want to keep moving."

"My sister is going to make us an offer," Hortense said. "I'm not sure we have much choice."

"I don't want to stay here," Henrietta said.

Hortense sighed, then kissed the top of Henrietta's head. "I have to help Lola with Cinderella."

When she was alone, Henrietta sat at the dressing table and studied MoMo's box. "Being dead must be like sleeping," she said after a while, as though she'd been giving the matter some thought. "You don't know you're alive when you're sleeping. You don't even know you're here."

She looked in the mirror and wished again that she could see her father looking back at her. She returned her attention to the box.

"When you're sleeping," she said, "you wake up. When you're dead, you don't, so it's like being asleep forever." She didn't know if what she was saying made any sense, but it sounded possible. It offered a strange kind of comfort.

"I'm going to do the Eight-Foot-Tall in Union Square," she said to MoMo's box. "Somehow."

There was a knock at the door. "Henrietta? You in there?" It was Ixnay. "I've got something to show you."

CARLOTTA'S OFFER

Here's one," Hortense said the next day.

"One what?" Henrietta asked. She knew exactly what her mother was talking about. It wasn't a subject she wanted to address. She'd woken up this morning not wanting to give an inch.

"A job," Hortense said, ignoring her daughter's mood. They were sitting in front of the RV. The first rehearsals of the day were over.

"Why are you looking for a job?" Henrietta's clown face was gone. She was still wearing the butterfly shirt.

Hortense looked around the corner of the local newspaper she was holding. "You have your father's perverse sense of humor." She smiled, then bit her lower lip.

"You can't place a dollar value on a good laugh," Henrietta said.

"So your father said."

"Corny humor is the best because it lasts the longest."

"His very words," Hortense said. "Do you remember everything he said?"

"I remember a lot," Henrietta said. "Sometimes the words just come out and it feels like him saying them."

"A job is how we pay the bills," Hortense said.

"You don't need a job," Henrietta said. "We're going to be a big hit in Union Square and then we'll do another performance and another."

"There's an ad for a receptionist at a dentist's office," was how her mother chose to respond. "I might be able to talk my way into that."

"No good," Henrietta said.

"Why is it no good?"

"Because of all the yelling and screaming."

"What yelling and screaming?"

"When they drill holes in your teeth."

"Nobody screams anymore," Hortense said.

"I do," Henrietta said.

Her mother laughed. The clowns had their teeth cleaned and worked on once a year by Doctor Dibble when they performed outside Oxnard, California. Doctor Dibble was an amateur clown, and he got to be in the show in exchange for his services.

"There are teaching jobs," Hortense said. "They always need replacements at the last minute. I'd have to get certified again. I'd have to go back to school and take some courses."

"You're too old for school," Henrietta said.

"Nobody is too old for school," Hortense said. "Not even you. I'd go nights. There's a college a few miles from here."

"Maybe we won't be here."

"I'm just exploring the possibilities."

"It's possible we'll be somewhere else," Henrietta said.

Hortense responded by returning her attention to the employment ads.

"Why won't they let you teach the way you are?" Henrietta asked. "You already teach me. Look how smart I am."

"I'll use you as my reference," Hortense said. "A private school is advertising for an English teacher. I won't need a state certification for that. Who am I kidding? I've been out of it too long. I'm a rusty old bucket."

"You don't look like a rusty old bucket to me," Henrietta said.

"Thank you. That's the nicest thing I've heard in a while."

"It gets cold here in the winter," Henrietta said.

"That's why they make warm clothes."

"I don't have any warm clothes."

"You would if you lived here."

"I don't live here," Henrietta said.

Hortense circled an ad.

❂　❂　❂

The afternoon flew by. Henrietta rehearsed with the other clowns, then got in some time with Ixnay rehearsing the Eight-Foot-Tall. It didn't go that well, but it was a beginning.

Ixnay said he'd do some fine-tuning. Henrietta said she could do better. When she returned to the RV, her mother told her to change her shirt.

"I'm out of patience," she said. "I want you to take that shirt off now."

"I'm going to the Laundromat tomorrow," Henrietta said. "I'll wash it then."

"Yesterday you said you'd change it today."

A knock at the door interrupted them. "I'll wait by the car," Fenimore called in.

"Wait for what?" Henrietta asked.

"We're having dinner at Carlotta's."

"You didn't tell me."

"I did."

"You didn't."

"I'm sure I did."

"I'm sure you didn't."

"I know I told you, Henrietta."

"I know you didn't."

"Okay," Hortense said, "maybe I didn't. Maybe I forgot and you don't know anything about it. You're still coming. And you're going to change that shirt. Don't take forever."

When her mother was gone, Henrietta sat at the makeup table. "Why do I have to do what I don't want to?" she asked MoMo's box. "Why did it have to happen? Why does it have to be like this?"

She marched to the Rolls-Royce in her butterfly shirt.

"This is how I'm going," she said. Her body was rigid with resistance.

Instead of getting upset, her mother said, "It's not easy for either of us."

Fenimore opened the door, and they climbed in.

❖   ❖   ❖

Carlotta led them into the large dining room, where they sat at a long table that was beneath an enormous glass chandelier. The walls held more of those paintings of people in old-fashioned clothes.

"Dining early is good for the digestive system," Carlotta said. She sat at the head of the table. Henrietta sat to her right, directly across from her mother.

"My digestive system is good all the time," Henrietta said, offering up a small burp to make the point.

"Young ladies don't do that," Carlotta said.

"I'm not a young lady," Henrietta said.

Carlotta turned to her sister. "When I told her she was pretty, she said the same thing."

"I'm not pretty and I'm not not pretty," Henrietta said. "I just am."

"You are an attractive young lady, whether you care for the idea or not," Carlotta said.

"I'm a clown," Henrietta said, prepared to do battle for the rest of the night.

"Life isn't a fairy tale." Carlotta delivered a meaningful glance at her sister. "You have a lot of catching up to do."

"Henrietta is a quick study," Hortense said. "She knows how to take care of herself."

The conversation came to a momentary halt.

Henrietta inspected her surroundings. She figured everybody from the circus could eat in the room. She'd never seen so many knives, forks, spoons, glasses, and plates. She put her napkin on her lap. The first course was soup.

"Consommé," Carlotta said as Fenimore served.

"Beef broth," Fenimore whispered as he ladled some into Henrietta's bowl.

"There's nothing in it," Henrietta whispered back.

"It's better for you this way," Carlotta said.

Henrietta was impressed with her aunt's hearing. She'd have to remember that. She tasted it. It wasn't bad, but she liked the way Ixnay made soup better, with chunks of vegetables and noodles and sometimes meat.

"What have you done about placing Henrietta in school?" Carlotta asked her sister.

"We've been busy," Hortense said.

"It begins right after Labor Day," Carlotta said.

"I know when it starts," Hortense said.

"I wouldn't put it off," Carlotta said. She directed her attention to Henrietta. "I'm sure you're bright and will do well."

"I go to school at the circus," Henrietta said.

"How are the schools here?" Hortense asked.

"No better or worse than most, I'd imagine," Carlotta

said. "I don't know what they teach these days. You should go back to it. You should never have stopped."

"All my teachers are clowns," Henrietta said. "I'll be put in first grade."

"I know it will be difficult at first," Carlotta said, "but you'll do what you have to, like the rest of us."

Fenimore removed the bowls and served the next course, which was crab cakes about the size of silver dollars. He served Henrietta five.

"You have decisions to make," Carlotta said to her sister. "They have to be made now."

"I know," Hortense said. "There's a lot to consider."

"I wouldn't think that much," Carlotta said. "It's not as though you have anywhere else to go."

"We can go wherever we want," Henrietta said. "Our house has wheels."

"It's been hard to concentrate," Hortense said.

"You don't have to take it all on your shoulders," Carlotta said. "We can do it together."

Fenimore returned with the main course, braised rabbit with onions.

"I won't eat a rabbit," Henrietta said when she found out what it was.

"Make believe it's a chicken," Carlotta said. "It tastes a lot like that."

"But I already know it's a rabbit," Henrietta said.

"It's delicious," Hortense said.

"You won't like me any better than you liked my father," Henrietta said to her aunt.

Her mother gave her a withering look. Henrietta decided she'd said enough. Her rabbit remained untouched. Hortense asked Carlotta about the nearby college. Henrietta tuned them out. She counted the paintings of the people in old-fashioned clothes. There were sixteen of them. She tried to count the separate pieces of glass in the chandelier but kept losing track somewhere about one hundred and forty-seven. Fenimore wheeled a cart into the room.

"Crêpes suzette," Carlotta said to Henrietta. "I thought you'd enjoy seeing them made."

Fenimore lit an alcohol burner. He mixed ingredients in a saucepan, brought them to a boil over the burner's flame, added liquid from a brown bottle, then lit the contents with a match. Flame shot into the air, burned brightly, then faded out. Fenimore dipped a thin pancake into the bubbling sauce with a fork. He turned it over, then folded it onto a plate. He added another, then spooned sauce over both and served Carlotta. He made two for Hortense and three for Henrietta, who could taste lemon and orange and sugar and butter as each bite melted in her mouth. Fenimore served coffee.

"You might like to go with Fenimore to the kitchen," Carlotta said. "I'm sure you'll have more fun."

"It would be better if I stayed," Henrietta said.

"It's her life too," Hortense said.

"If that's how you want it," Carlotta said. "I don't know

what's going on these days. I want the two of you to live with me. It's a big house. Part of it can be turned into an apartment with its own entrance."

"I can sing and dance and juggle and ride a unicycle," Henrietta said. "I can walk on stilts and do magic and tumble." She felt these things had to be said. She got up, walked across the room on her hands, flipped to her feet, and sat again.

Carlotta applauded. "It's going to be wonderful having you here," she said. "All your energy filling the place." She turned to Hortense. "I'll have Fenimore get your rooms ready and arrange things with a contractor to get started. If you need money in the meantime, you'll please be kind enough to tell me."

"I don't know what to say," Hortense said.

"You don't have to say anything," Carlotta said. "You'll see how much easier things are from now on."

"I don't know what to say," Hortense said again.

Henrietta couldn't tell if her mother was accepting the offer, or hadn't really decided. She wanted them to get up and leave and not come back.

"It's a very generous offer," Hortense said.

"Then it's settled," Carlotta said.

Henrietta's heart sank.

GROWING UP

Henrietta didn't notice right away because the green and black striped shorts she put on were baggy and long to begin with, and she hadn't yet washed away the cobwebs of sleep. But her mother noticed. Hortense was watching unhappily as her daughter buttoned the butterfly shirt.

"You're taller," Hortense said as it registered.

"I am?" Henrietta made it sound like she'd just heard something that was impossible.

"Stand against the wall." Hortense went for the tape measure.

"How could I be taller than yesterday?" Henrietta pressed her back against the place where earlier lines had been drawn. The last one was from a year ago.

"Stand straight." Hortense marked her daughter's new height with a pencil, measured, then looked her up and down. "Two and a half inches. Like a volcano rising up out of the ocean overnight."

"I grew two and a half inches while I was sleeping?" Henrietta didn't sound happy about it.

"You are now officially four feet, five and one half inches tall," Hortense said.

"I don't want to grow. I liked it the way I was."

"You were never going to stay the same as your father," she said. "You know that."

"I want to be like him."

"You *are* like him. And me. And most of all yourself. Who you are won't change because you grow."

Henrietta noticed the sleeves of the butterfly shirt had climbed nearly to her wrists. She rolled them up to her elbows.

"We'll get you new clothes after Union Square," Hortense said. "You can get by until then."

"What about my costumes?"

"You'll get one more performance out of them. If that shirt isn't washed today, you'll have to peel it off with a paint scraper."

"I'm going to the Laundromat with Sweetpea," Henrietta said. "How much more will I grow?"

"I don't know," Hortense said, "but it will be exactly the right height for you."

Henrietta had to admit that being taller didn't make her feel any different. So maybe it was true that she wouldn't be any different. And it wasn't as though she had anything to say about it anyway. Lately she'd come to understand how few choices she had. Her legs looked longer as she studied them. Her flip-flops still fit.

Her mother hadn't said anything about Carlotta's offer. Not last night after Fenimore drove them back from dinner. Not this morning, and the day's rehearsals had already begun. Henrietta hoped it was because she hadn't made up her mind yet. If she hadn't, it meant there was still time. Until her mother told her they were staying, they were free.

Henrietta found Ixnay cleaning the truck's spark plugs. "I grew last night," she said. "I won't be eight feet tall when I do the act. I'll be eight feet, two and a half inches."

"I can fix that," Ixnay said. He pulled two small bottles of chocolate soda pop from his cooler, opened them, and handed one to Henrietta.

"I might grow more," Henrietta said.

"Just don't do it before the performance," Ixnay said.

"What are you going to do after the circus closes?" Henrietta asked.

"We're going back to Massachusetts," Ixnay said. "I'm going to open a garage. No gas. Repairs and tune-ups only. How are you and your mom doing?"

"We're okay," Henrietta said with more confidence than she was feeling. She told Ixnay about Carlotta and her fear that they'd end up living here. "It's not that she's a terrible person. I just don't want to stay."

"Maybe it won't happen," Ixnay said. "Don't worry too much. We may think we know what's going to happen next, but we don't."

Henrietta thought those were the truest words she'd ever heard.

"I was married once," Ixnay said. "We were in our twenties. She died from cancer. You always keep the sadness, but what you remember are the happy things, and they make you feel better."

Henrietta rehearsed the Eight-Foot-Tall for an hour. She made substantial progress. Ixnay said he'd make more adjustments. They still had no idea if it would be successful.

Next Henrietta went in search of Wilhelmenia, who was oiling her roller skates. "I'm taller," she said.

"A couple of inches," Wilhelmenia said.

"Two and a half. What are you going to do after Union Square?"

"We're going back to Pittsburgh," Wilhelmenia said. "We have a house there. My cousin owns a cocktail lounge. I'm going to sing and play the keyboard. Grandmother Spangle will do the lights."

"What about Sweetpea?"

"She'll go to school. You'll have to ask her the rest of it."

Henrietta talked to Wilhelmenia a while longer, then went to see Guillermo and Lola. They were dancing the tango behind their RV. Henrietta informed them of her new height.

"It suits you," Lola told her.

"We're rehearsing," Guillermo said.

"We're opening a dance studio for seniors in Florida," Lola said.

They flashed their brilliant smiles and tangoed on.

Henrietta found Grouchy and Notz playing chess. "It's Plastic Woman," Grouchy said, seeing the difference right away.

"Two and a half inches," Henrietta said.

"It shows," Notz said.

She asked them what they were going to do.

"I'm going to find me a nine-to-five job that produces a paycheck every Friday," Notz said, "along with health benefits and weekends off."

"I'm going to write a book about Filbert's," Grouchy said.

"You're going to need a day job while you're doing it," Notz said.

"I'm expecting you and Ixnay to support the artist in the family," Grouchy said.

"We'll support you right out the front door if you don't pay your share of the rent," Notz said. He winked at Henrietta.

After a lunch of bologna and cheese sandwiches, coleslaw, potato chips, and iced tea, Henrietta and Sweetpea headed for town, each pulling a cart of laundry.

"I'm taller," Henrietta said.

"Not much," Sweetpea said.

"Two and a half inches."

"You're still a kid."

"I'll keep growing."

"Eventually," Sweetpea said. "Someday."

"Are you afraid of going to school?" Henrietta asked.

"Why would I be afraid? I want to go."

"I'm afraid."

"Of what? Nobody can do half the stuff you can. You're smart."

"What if I don't like it? What do I do then? It will be like jail."

"You're crazy," Sweetpea said. "Millions of kids go to school. I'm going to college someday. A good one. You make more money if you do that. Grandmother Spangle says you and your mother are going to live here with your aunt."

"I don't know," Henrietta said. She started walking faster. She didn't want to talk about it.

"What do you mean, you don't know?"

"I don't know," Henrietta yelled. "That's what I mean." She stopped at the corner. Sweetpea started across the street.

"Come back!" Henrietta shouted. "The light is red."

"No cars are coming," Sweetpea said.

"Come back!" Henrietta's voice carried even more urgency this time. "Hurry."

"Oh, all right." Sweetpea returned to the sidewalk and waited for the light to change. "It's not so bad here," she said. "You might like it."

"How could I like it? You don't know what you're talking about." The WALK sign flashed. Henrietta looked both ways, then hurried to the other side, pulling the cart behind her. How could she live where her father had been killed? She ignored Sweetpea the rest of the way.

They set themselves up by a window. Henrietta stripped to her T-shirt and added the butterfly shirt to her load.

"Now that I'm not going to be a clown anymore, it's starting to feel sad," Sweetpea said.

"Keep being a clown then," Henrietta said.

"Why would I do that?"

"So you wouldn't start to feel sad."

"You're not easy to talk to," Sweetpea said.

"If we sell out the show at Union Square, would you be willing to do one more after that?" Henrietta asked.

"What would be the point?"

"To keep going," Henrietta said, getting exasperated. "How are we going to live without the circus? Without being together all the time?"

"That's why it's sad, you idiot!" Sweetpea was upset now. Her cheeks were turning red. "I didn't say I wasn't going to miss it. I just said I don't want to do it anymore. None of us does, except you." She got up and left without saying where she was going.

Henrietta admitted to herself that the likelihood of the circus continuing on after Union Square was nil. Sweetpea was telling the truth. The other clowns had places to go and things they could do. She tried, but she couldn't imagine not being a clown. Then she thought she could stay one anyway. Her father had been a mime. He'd been a clown in restaurants. He'd been a professional wrestler. Henrietta thought she could do any of those things if she had to. And there were birthday parties and other occasions. A clown could do okay. And someday she could join a circus again.

140

Sweetpea returned with two ice cream cones. She held them both out to Henrietta. "Chocolate or chocolate chip?"

"I don't want any," Henrietta said, eyeing the chocolate. She was still annoyed.

"You have to learn how to talk to people," Sweetpea said. She bit into the chocolate chip.

Henrietta took the chocolate.

"It's my birthday today," Sweetpea said.

"I forgot," Henrietta said.

"Everybody forgot," Sweetpea said, "even my mother and grandmother. It's because of what happened to MoMo and us closing. I'm sixteen."

The first thing Henrietta did when she got back was to tell her mother she didn't want to live with Carlotta, but if that was what was decided, she'd go along, even though she thought it was a bad idea.

"I can make the decision for both of us and you'll be okay with it?" Hortense asked. "Even if it's to stay here?"

"Yes," Henrietta said. She'd decided it was a lot like the

blue shirt. Then she told her mother about it being Sweetpea's birthday. Hortense was horrified that they'd forgotten.
She rushed off to tell Wilhelmenia, who was even more
horrified and quickly organized a shopping expedition. The
festivities got under way after dinner.

141

DECISIONS

unday was the day Henrietta had to decide about doing the Eight-Foot-Tall. She put it to the test. She fastened the breakaway straps Ixnay had made from canvas and Velcro. They joined her feet to the aluminum tubes Ixnay had fashioned into stilts. He'd created knee joints from heavy springs, but they could move only a little. She held on to the side of the truck and pulled herself upright. Ixnay had cut two and a half inches off the tubes and re-attached the pads that served as feet. She stood exactly eight feet tall.

Henrietta could walk, run, stop short, turn, and dance without effort. Her balance was flawless, just as it had been atop her father's shoulders. The trouble came when she tried the more daring moves. Each time she tried to bend too far, or swoop about in some manner, she fell. At the end, she managed only a somersault and a half and landed on her backside. She rehearsed until she was able to complete two full somersaults and land on her feet.

"Nobody will think the worse of you if you decide not to do it," Ixnay said.

"I am going to do it," Henrietta said. She knew she couldn't do the whole act, but she could manage some of it. A few of the moves would work if she kept the audience focused on her face and arms and upper body. She'd sell it if she kept it brief. And if she made a pinpoint landing.

"MoMo told me it would all come together when we got there," she said. "He told me to trust myself."

"Then that's exactly what you should do," Ixnay said.

Henrietta and her mother did a final run-through of the mirror act. It went off without a hitch. Hortense said she was glad she'd been talked into it. Late that afternoon Carlotta came to see them.

"Why haven't I heard from you?" she asked the moment she stepped into the RV. "We should be making plans."

"We've been rehearsing," Hortense said.

"I've come to bring you back to the house," Carlotta said.

"We have to talk," Hortense said. "Sit down."

"Talk about what?" Carlotta sat on the couch. "Everything is decided."

Henrietta watched her mother sit on the bench at the makeup table. MoMo's box was only a few inches away. Henrietta slid to the floor, coming to rest near the door.

"I don't know how you did it all these years," Carlotta

said. "Always traveling. Having nothing of your own. You can hardly breathe in here."

"It was paradise when MoMo was alive," Hortense said.

Carlotta nodded. "It was hard when I lost Barnaby. I knew I'd never find anybody else."

"This has been my home for thirteen years," Hortense said.

"Fenimore will sell it for you," Carlotta said, "but I don't think you'll get much."

Henrietta clenched her teeth together to keep herself from screaming, *No!* Fenimore would *not* sell the RV. Nobody would. Not ever. But she'd told her mother to make the decision and she would honor it. She meant to keep her promise, no matter how difficult it would be.

"We're not staying," Hortense said.

Three words. Just like that. Henrietta's mouth nearly dropped open. Had she heard correctly? Was her mother saying no? She saw her aunt Carlotta go rigid.

"It has nothing to do with you," Hortense continued. "We appreciate your offer. I'm glad we're back in each other's lives. But Henrietta and I have to do something on our own."

Her mother was saying no. Henrietta wanted to jump up and cheer. She was barely able to stay still.

"You're running away again," Carlotta said, getting to her feet.

"We're not running," Hortense said, "we're looking. There's a difference."

"What are you going to do? Join another circus? Live like this for the rest of your life? Is that what you want? You want you daughter to grow up to be a clown?" Carlotta's voice rose as she spoke. She was struggling to keep her composure.

"We'll find a place," Hortense said. "I'll go back to teaching. Henrietta will go to school. If she wants to be a clown after that, it's okay with me."

"You can do all that here," Carlotta said. "I have everything ready. Whatever you need I can provide."

"We can't," Hortense said. "I'm sorry."

"You always did what you wanted," Carlotta said, sounding nasty now. "You're selfish. All you think about is yourself. I don't care what you do." She headed for the door, looking down at Henrietta as she passed.

"You're too much like your father," she said.

"That's the best thing anybody ever said about me," Henrietta replied. She watched Fenimore help her aunt into the back of the Rolls-Royce. Her mother moved into the doorway as they drove off.

"Are you all right?" Henrietta asked.

"I am," Hortense said. "Are you?"

"I am," she said. "Is it really okay if I stay a clown?"

"If you finish school first."

Henrietta felt some of the heaviness she'd been carrying leave her body. She looked up at her mother. "How come you changed your mind about living here?"

"Who said I wanted to live here?"

"I thought you did."

"I guess I did," Hortense said. "I had this idea that we'd all come back and live near her when the circus closed. Be a larger family. Then after what happened, I thought staying was the only thing we could do."

"What happened?"

"You happened," she said. "When you told me I could decide for both of us, I started thinking maybe we should have an adventure instead. To see what we can make of ourselves."

THE FUTURE

The day began with breakfast and a meeting. Nobody said anything about it being the last time they'd gather like this. Henrietta did her best to make believe it was a morning like all other mornings. While the clowns consumed scrambled eggs and those little sausages that look like pudgy baby fingers, Wilhelmenia went over the drill for Union Square. They'd set up as soon as they got there. After the performance, they'd go their separate ways.

"We're not going to make a big deal out of saying goodbye," she said. "We'll stay in touch. We'll see each other. Let's think about tonight. Let's put on the greatest show in the history of Filbert's Traveling Clown Circus."

"For MoMo," the clowns yelled.

The equipment was divided equally among the clowns according to their needs and desires. They'd take what they'd chosen after the show. When the meeting was over,

Henrietta went from RV to RV to pay each of her friends a final visit. Everybody was packing up. The conversations were brief. She asked each of them for something personal to remember them by.

 From Ixnay, Grouchy, and Notz she got hats. From Lola and Guillermo, a pair of dancing shoes. From Grandmother Spangle, the journal she'd been keeping for the past year, knowing they were the circus's last days. The final entry would be made tonight, and Grandma Spangle would give it to her then. From Wilhelmenia, a photograph of MoMo and Filbert in costume. Filbert was six feet seven and thin as a pole. Sweetpea gave her a small painting of a clown she'd done when she was six.

"You're going to have an interesting life," Sweetpea said. "You're different from the rest of us. The way MoMo was."

Henrietta packed her gifts into one of the costume trunks. She secured MoMo's box to the makeup table with the bungee cords Ixnay had provided. "Better than a seat belt," she said. She rested her hands on the box. Doing so every time she was near it had already become habit.

The detective came while they were eating lunch. He had nothing new to report. He asked Hortense to let him know where they were so he could reach them. He told them they wouldn't give up looking for the driver of that car.

"Where are we going?" Henrietta asked her mother when the detective was gone.

"Pick a direction," Hortense said. "South or west?"

"West."

"West it is. Any part of it in particular?"

"I don't know," Henrietta said.

"Then how about we look until we both agree," Hortense said. "But we can't take too long. Our money won't last more than a month."

Henrietta nodded. It sounded like a plan to her.

The clowns cleaned up, stowed the folding chairs and tables, and started their RVs. One after the other they snaked free from the circle and made their way to the street. Ixnay's truck brought up the rear.

Henrietta saw the Rolls-Royce coming up behind them in the mirror. She watched it pull alongside. Fenimore honked the horn and waved. Hortense braked to a stop. Carlotta got out of the car. Hortense climbed down from the RV. Henrietta climbed down after her.

"I'm sorry about yesterday," Carlotta said. "There must be some way we can make up for the past."

"I'll let you know where we are," Hortense said. "You can come see us."

"I will," Carlotta said. "And you'll visit me here."

"When we've gotten ourselves organized," Hortense said.

Henrietta wasn't sure she ever wanted to come back, but that was a long way off. She'd worry about it when she had to.

"If you need money, don't be a fool about it," Carlotta said. "I have more than I need."

"I won't be a fool," Hortense said.

"Good," Carlotta said, "then you'll take this." She handed Hortense an envelope. Before her sister could object, she embraced her.

"We'll get this right eventually," she said, then broke free and started for the car. She returned suddenly, like she'd forgotten something. This time she addressed Henrietta.

"Take care of your mother," she said.

"I will," Henrietta said.

"She's lucky to have you." Carlotta gave her a long look, leaned forward, planted a kiss on her cheek, then moved quickly to the car and got in.

Fenimore said goodbye to Hortense. He offered Henrietta his hand. "I haven't heard the last of you," he said. He drove Carlotta off with a wave.

The caravan proceeded to a discount gas station, where Wilhelmenia told the clowns to fill up. She was paying. She said she wished she could do more. She handed out directions to Union Square, in case anybody fell behind. She led the caravan to Route 25A, then west toward New York City.

Henrietta kept adjusting herself in the passenger seat. It felt strange riding in it. She glanced back at MoMo's box.

"We're going to talk about Mark Twain," Hortense said.

"He wrote the story about the jumping frogs."

"His real name was Samuel Clemens," Hortense said. "Mark Twain was the name he used for his books."

"Why didn't he use his real name?"

"Maybe he felt more like somebody named Mark Twain than somebody named Samuel Clemens."

"I'm always going to use my real name. What else did he write about besides jumping frogs?"

"Sometimes he wrote about children who got into trouble. Sometimes he wrote about children who had to make big decisions. I picked one of his books up at the used bookstore in Oyster Bay. It's called *Huckleberry Finn*."

"What's it about?"

"It's about learning that everything we're taught isn't necessarily so," Hortense said. "And that sometimes doing the right thing means going against the rules. It's also an adventure. We'll read it together while we're traveling. Meanwhile, we'll talk about Mr. Twain."

Class was in session. Henrietta listened happily. She loved how her mother made something more interesting than it already was.

They drove through Roslyn and Great Neck, then entered Queens. They made their way onto the Grand Central Parkway and drove past Flushing Bay and LaGuardia Airport. Henrietta watched a plane lifting off the ground and wondered where it was going. They drove beneath elevated train tracks, then onto the Queensboro Bridge, which spanned the East River at Fifty-ninth Street and emptied into Manhattan.

She heard calliope music burst forth from the speaker on top of Wilhelmenia's RV. She heard Grandmother Spangle's voice announcing that this would be Filbert's Traveling Clown Circus's one and only appearance in New York City.

Suddenly Henrietta was crying. For her father. For her mother. For herself. For the time that was gone and would never come back. She'd never see MoMo again. But she had his words, and all that she'd learned from the years they'd spent together.

152

"You'd be all right," her father had told her when she'd asked him about being afraid. "You know how to look something in the eye and take care of it."

Henrietta glanced at her mother and saw that her expression was set with purpose. She knew somehow they'd be all right. She decided that there would be three Hornbuckles, always three. No matter what. She wiped at her tears.

"We're going to do boffo," she said.